This book was inspired
by Hans Christian Andersen, greatest
storyteller of the Nineteenth Century, and
Ruth Sawyer, greatest storyteller of the
Twentieth Century.

Fairystories are meant to be heard with
ear and heart, not read with the eye.
Andersen knew that. His first fairytales did
not enter dressed in emperor's clothes,
accompanied by colored illustrations. They
were published cheaply, in a 61-page booklet,
when he was 30 years old. The literary critics
greeted the tales with silence or mockery. But
Andersen, better than they, knew the path
into the fantasy world of children. He
explained simply: "I wanted the style to be
such that the reader felt the presence of the
storyteller; therefore the spoken language
had to be used."

Ralt's Stories

Princes, Monsters and Magic

Crafted by
Ralph Wallenhorst

DRAGON TALE PRESS
MADEIRA BEACH, FL

Cover illustration Copyright 1984 by John Horrall.
Front and back plates by Lonni Lees Brooker.
Poems on pages 8-9 Copyright 1980 by Edward F. Sundberg.
Newspaper story on page 123 Copyright 1985 by the St. Petersburg
Times. Reprinted with permission.

Published by the Ruth Sawyer Memorial Foundation, Post Office
Box 86255, Madeira Beach, FL 33738. Distributed by Dragon Tale
Press, a division of the Foundation. Printed in the United States of
America by McNaughton & Gunn, Inc.

First printing   September 1989
Second printing   October 1990

Library of Congress Cataloging-in-Publication Data

Wallenhorst, Ralph, 1917-
    Ralf's stories : princes, monsters and magic / crafted by Ralph
Wallenhorst.
        p.   cm.
    Includes bibliographical references.
    Summary: Presents a collection of traditional and original
fairy and folk tales suitable for reading aloud.
    ISBN 0-9622905-0-5 : $12.00 -- ISBN 0-9622905-1-3 (pbk.) : $6.00
    1. Fairy tales. 2. Tales. [1. Fairy tales. 2. Folklore.]
I. Title.
PZ8.W173 Ral 1989
[398.2]--dc20   89-38025

Contents

Hi!

I'm Ralf The Storyteller.

Will you let me be one of your friends?

I go from city to city, telling stories. So far I've been to more than 400 schools. But it may be a long time until I can get to yours.

So I've written down some of the tales other children like best. Here they are. I hope you like them too.

Take your time when you read. Imagine what the people looked like. How they dressed. How they talked. Some were sweet and gentle, like the fairy Thumbelina. Some were mean, like the fat king in "The King's Flea." He deserved what happened to him.

You'll find lots of dragons in this book. That's because I think dragons are neat. One dragon doesn't have anything to do with the stories. It's on the cover. I put it there because I liked it. I think it looks the way a dragon ought to look.

Remember to tell your friends which stories you liked best so they can read them too. Or maybe you can get your teacher or parents to use this book for storyhours.

While you're exploring, here's another idea—ask your parents what stories they loved when they were your age.

Have a happy time.

Ralf

The old Viking grave
Guards the fjord ... The breezes
Sing so peacefully.

By Edward F. Sundberg. Reprinted, with
permission, from "Temper Not The Wind."

When early spring comes
I dream of sleek dragon ships
Slicing the cool seas...

The King's Flea

Long ago when kings ruled the world, there lived in Spain a king who loved to trick people. He thought he was very funny—but all he really was was very fat. Above all, he loved telling dumb riddles. Some he made up himself. You could tell from his fat grin when he thought he'd invented a good riddle.

This was his favorite. When you visited his palace, you'd find him sitting on his golden throne. He would hold out a pack of cards to you. He'd tap the deck with his fat fingers, squint his eyelids, and demand: "When you play cards here, how many kings are there?"

If you were like me, you'd answer: "Four—the king of clubs, the king of diamonds, the king of hearts, and the king of spades."

Then he'd laugh and slap his leg and roar: "WRONG! Five kings. The king of clubs and the king of diamonds and the king of hearts and the king of spades . . . and the King Of Spain!"

Well, don't you think that was a dumb riddle? But it's the kind of riddle he loved.

Now for our story.

One day the king of Spain was sitting on his

throne, petting his pet dog, when a flea jumped off the dog's back. A flea is a little bug, like a mosquito without any stinger. Anyhow, this flea landed on the back of the king's hand.

The king made a cup out of his other hand and clapped it over the flea. He raised the cupped hand a little, peeked under, then shut the hand down again. "Por Dios!" he grinned. "A flea! Whoever heard of a king with a pet flea? Ah, this will fool people!"

He summoned the captain of his soldiers. "Now that we have this impertinent flea, what shall we do with it?"

The captain tried desperately to guess what the king had in mind. He saluted and said: "Make up a firing squad? Execute it?"

The king roared: "NO, STUPID! Put it in a cage, a great glass cage. Feed it every hour. Let us just see how big it will grow."

So that's what they did.

At the end of a month, the flea was as big as a rat. In another month, big as a cat. The king pointed at the flea and shouted: "I name you . . . Felipa!"

The king's grown daughter, the Princess Belita, protested: "Daddy! When you were a little boy, didn't you have a nurse named Felipa?"

The king sniffed: "I certainly did. She's still alive. And she's just as ugly as this big flea. So, in her honor, I'm naming this flea Felipa. Ho, ho, ho!"

In another month, the flea was big as a dog. And in another month, big as a baby sheep.

But then the flea stopped growing.

The king had his soldiers kill Felipa. The flea's skin was stretched and soaked in milk until it was as soft as silk. Then Princess Belita had it made into a tambourine, which is a kind of musical instrument like the top of a small drum. With it the princess learned to dance very prettily, rattling the tambourine over her head and stamping her heels.

The king invited in his noblemen, one by one. He announced he had a new riddle for them. Then Princess Belita would dance while the king would roar out:

> *"Belita—Felipa—they dance well together.*
> *Belita—Felipa—now answer me whether*
> *You know this Felipa, this animalita . . .*
> *If you answer right, you MARRY BELITA!"*

Well, those noblemen knew what tambourines are usually made of. So they'd say: "The skin of a goat, your majesty." Or "The skin of a sheep, your majesty."

Then the king would shout "WRONG!" and make them give the princess a new gown for not guessing his riddle. As you can imagine, soon her closets were crowded with new dresses.

Everywhere the Princess Belita went, she would flutter her eyelashes and go tap-tap-tap with her fingertips on the tambourine. Now, you know how a noise like that gets on everybody's nerves, even a king's. But this king couldn't quite make up his mind what he wanted to happen. He would have liked somebody to marry Princess Belita and take her away, so he'd be free of that constant tapping. But he hated to think anyone was smart enough to guess his riddle.

Finally he put up signs inviting anyone in the kingdom to come and try. But anybody who guessed wrong would be hanged. So not many people took the chance. Would you?

However, far back in the mountains of Castile there lived a young shepherd named Manuelito. He had heard how beautiful the Princess Belita was. So he announced he was going to try.

His mother shook her finger under his nose and told him: "Son, you are a fool. How can you guess the king's riddle? Why, you cannot even read or write. Stay here at home and save yourself a hanging."

But Manuelito folded his arms and was stubborn.

So his mother sighed, gave him her blessing, and baked him a tortilla to carry for tomorrow's breakfast.

He put it in his pouch and off he went.

After he'd walked a ways, he sat down in the dusty path to rest. A little grey mouse hopped out of the bushes, sat up on his hind legs, and squeaked: "Please, senor. Put me in your pouch and give me a ride to the king's palace."

Manuelito asked why he wanted to go that far.

The mouse explained: "I can steal more food in the king's kitchen than I can find out here in the fields."

Manuelito grinned at the sassy answer. Then he shook his head. "I am sorry, Senor Mouse. I already have a tortilla in my pouch. If I put you in too, tomorrow morning my tortilla will taste like a mouse."

The mouse said: "That makes sense. But why wait? Eat the tortilla now."

Well, you know how hungry you get walking. So Manuelito ate the tortilla.

As he wiped the last crumbs from his lips, the mouse said: "You see? Now the pouch is empty. So put me in."

Manuelito did.

Finally, the next afternoon, they arrived at the palace. Manuelito sat down outside, under a tree. The mouse called out through the pouch skin: "Well? Well? What are we waiting for?"

Manuelito said: "I have to guess the answer to a hard riddle. If I can't, the king will hang me."

The mouse said: "Oh, that. I'll help you. Let's get going. It's hot inside this pouch."

So Manuelito climbed the palace steps. He told the guard he had come to answer the king's riddle.

The guard looked down at him and said "Pobrecito!" (That's Spanish. You pronounce it "pohb-pray-seeto" and it means "poor little wretch.")

The guard passed Manuelito on to the footman. He said "Pobrecito!" and waved Manuelito along. The chief of the king's bodyguard shook his head at the ragged boy, said "Pobrecito," and took him on to the royal dining room. The king was just sitting down with the princess.

The king didn't say "Pobrecito!" No, he said: "BOY, YOU LOOK THIN AS A STICK. Sit down and have a good meal with us."

So Manuelito tried. There were 14 kinds of food on silver platters. But delicious as all that food looked, Manuelito only poked at it with his fork. He just wasn't hungry. Can you guess what he was worrying might happen—something that could spoil anybody's appetite?

After supper was over, the king said: "You look like a nice lad. Why don't you just go home to your sheep? Life as a shepherd is better than no life at all."

Manuelito frowned and said: "No. I want my chance. I've dreamed of seeing the Princess Belita dance."

The king shrugged. "Have it your own way." Then a smile spread slowly across his face. "Anyhow, I did have my heart set on hanging somebody today. Might as well be you."

So Princess Belita danced, her tambourine clattering, her skirt flying and her heels hammering the floor. The king roared out:

"Belita—Felipa—they dance well together.
Belita—Felipa—now answer me whether
You know this Felipa, this animalita . . .
    If you answer right, you marry Belita!"

When the princess stopped to catch her breath, Manuelito strode over and took the tambourine from her. He tapped it. He smelled it. He tasted it with his tongue. Finally he said in a puzzled voice: "I know what goatskin is like, and what sheepskin is like. This is neither one. But—but—I don't have any idea what it really is."

He thought and thought.

The king said: "Well? Well? We can't sit here all night. Make your guess and let's get on with the hanging."

Now, all this time the mouse had been chewing away at the inside of Manuelito's pouch. Finally he gnawed a hole. Through that hole the mouse fell, out of the pouch and onto the tambourine.

The king stared at Manuelito in delight. "You're a magician! What a wonderful trick! You *grew* a mouse on the tambourine."

Princess Belita screamed and got up on top of the table.

"Phew!" said the mouse. "Why did you drop me?"

Manuelito picked up the mouse. He held it close to his cheek, stroked its fur gently, and said: "Don't be scared, little mouse. It's not you they're going to hang."

The mouse sneezed and said: "Phew. It was hot in there. But why did you drop me on that tambourine? It smells like a flea."

Manuelito grew very quiet. "A flea? Are you sure?"

"Of course I'm sure. Shouldn't I know what a flea smells like? Don't they bite me often enough?"

Manuelito turned to the princess and the king. He made a deep bow, held out the tambourine, and announced: "Your majesties. This tambourine—this Felipa—is made from the skin . . . of a flea."

This time the king couldn't shout: "WRONG! Guards, take him out and hang him."

Instead, he had to grump: "Right. You get to marry Belita."

But do you think the princess liked that—marry a poor shepherd boy with nothing to his name but a pet mouse?

She said: "Immmmpossible! I'll grant you a favor instead. Ask for anything you want—anything I own."

When Manuelito hesitated, the king said: "Come, come, lad. I'll grant you a second wish. What will it be? Would you like to carry a sword and be a captain of soldiers?"

Manuelito thought of all the marching soldiers do. He told the king: "No, thanks. I got tired just walking here. But princess—you ride in a beautiful carriage. Let me have that carriage to ride home in."

An evil grin began to creep across the king's face.

The mouse tugged frantically at Manuelito's shirt. Manuelito bent over and the mouse whispered in his ear.

Manuelito looked at the princess and added: "And six white horses to pull it."

The king's grin faded.

As for Princess Belita—do you think she agreed to give Manuelito what he asked for? Of course she did. She even gave him something extra—the tambourine to remember the day by.

The king clapped his hands and said: "Enough! Now, lad, what shall I give you?"

The mouse whispered in Manuelito's ear again.

Manuelito climbed into the princess' carriage and stood up. He said: "Your majesty, I have guessed your riddle after all your wise noblemen failed. If people see me coming home with nothing but this carriage, they will call you a cheapskate. So just fill my little pouch here with gold. But you must promise to fill it right up to the top."

The king said: "That little pouch? No sooner said than done." He snapped his fingers at the soldiers and pointed to the royal treasure room.

The soldiers dragged in a big chest of gold pieces. They began pouring them into Manuelito's pouch.

But you remember what was in the bottom of that pouch—the hole the mouse had chewed.

So as fast as the soldiers poured gold pieces into the top of Manuelito's pouch, down through that hole the heavy coins fell. They piled up in a shining heap around Manuelito's feet.

When the first treasure chest was empty, Manuelito slapped the side of his flat purse and told the king: "You see? Still not full."

The soldiers pulled in another chest and poured

that gold into Manuelito's pouch. But do you think those coins filled up the pouch, like the king had promised? Not with that hole still in the pouch.

So the soldiers poured . . . and poured . . . and poured. Until the king's treasury was nearly empty. And the carriage was filled with gold right up to Manuelito's knees.

Finally Manuelito said: "That's enough." After all, he didn't want the carriage to break, carrying all that heavy gold.

Manuelito put the mouse in his pocket. He kissed the king on the hand and the princess on the cheek. Then he climbed back into the carriage and sat on top of the big pile of gold. He whipped up the six horses and off he drove, back toward his own village.

As he became smaller and smaller in the distance, the princess and king could hear him tapping the tambourine and singing:

> *"Belita, Felipa, they dance well together—*
> *You take this Felipa,*
> *She's not made of leather.*
> *I guessed she's a flea. Hurray for me!*
> *Thanks, king, for the riddle.*
> *Adios, senorita!"*

At last Manuelito was out of sight.

The king looked down at all his empty treasure chests. Then he put his head down on his folded arms and cried. Never again in his life, he swore, would he make up another dumb riddle. Never!

But do you think he kept that promise?

THE SNAKE

In ancient days there lived a shepherd named Basil. One day, while tending his sheep, he heard a strange hissing sound from the forest. He ran to see what it was.

The dry grass and fallen leaves were burning. On a tree, in the center of the fire, was coiled a snake. It hissed: "Ssshepherd, sssave me from these flames."

Basil stretched his staff across the fire. The snake slid along the staff, across his hand, up his arm and around his neck.

Basil gasped: "Do not strangle me! I have helped you."

The snake answered: "Trussst me. Carry me home to my father, King of the Snakes. He will reward you."

Basil set off through the woods. Soon they came to a gateway formed entirely of snakes twisted around each other. The snake around Basil's neck commanded them: "Sssspread apart!"

The doorway widened. Through it they made their way into the den of the King of the Snakes. The snake around Basil's neck—it was the Snake King's daughter—told how Basil had rescued her from the forest fire.

The King of the Snakes hissed to his daughter: "Bite him lightly on the ear."

Before Basil could move, he felt a prick like the jab of a pin. Then the snake around his neck unwound itself and slid away.

The Snake King said: "Man, we have given you the greatest treasure we possess. You have heard we serpents are very wise. It is true. For we understand the languages of all the animals. Now we have shared this gift with you. Use it wisely and it will serve you well."

The shepherd went back to his flock. He found he could understand what the sheep were bleating, and the songs of birds, and what the field mice were chattering to each other.

He quit being a shepherd and set out in the world.

The first night he stayed at an inn. It was so small it had only one bedroom. Basil had to share the bed with another young traveler.

In the middle of the night, Basil waked to hear the mice in the corner saying: "Too bad. They look like nice young men. But this inn is run by robbers. When they are sure these travelers are deep asleep, they will climb in, kill them, and take their money."

Basil stayed awake. In the middle of the night, he heard someone putting a ladder underneath their window.

He shook his companion, whispering: "Wake up! Robbers are going to come through the window."

They stood on each side of the window. As each robber crept through, Basil hit him over the head with his staff, and his companion stabbed him with his dagger. There were three robbers, and they killed them all.

Afterwards, Basil's companion asked: "How did you know they were coming?"

Basil started to say that he could understand the language of animals. Then he thought: Nobody will believe that. So he said instead: "I saw it in a dream."

His companion nodded. "You are a wise man, and a brave one. Join me."

He explained that he was a prince in disguise. His mother was dead. To take his mind off his sorrow, he had been going about the kingdom seeking adventure. Then his father, the king, married again. The new queen's name was Epiria. She was very beautiful. But the prince suspected that, underneath, she was an evil witch.

Next morning a messenger arrived. He told the prince: "The king wishes you to return to the palace. He and the queen miss you very much."

The prince told Basil: "Now I know they love me. When I marry and have a son, they will turn the kingdom over to me. It is our law."

The prince, Basil, and the messenger started back on horses. Now, there was a strange thing about the messenger. On each of his shoulders rode a black crow. Basil could hear them saying:

"Caw. When we come to the bridge, the messenger will cross first. He will cut the rope that holds the bridge up. When the prince tries to cross, the bridge will collapse. He will be killed. Caw, caw. We know, but if any human tells what we have said, he will turn to stone from his toes to his waist."

At noon they stopped for lunch. Basil made an excuse and rode on ahead. He cut the bridge rope himself and then rode back.

That afternoon they all came to the bridge. The messenger started across. The prince would have followed him, but Basil put a hand on the horse's bridle and said: "Wait."

*Illustration by
Suzan Lovett*

Basil wondered if he could trust Queen Epiria.

When the messenger reached the center of the bridge, the planks gave way with a terrible crash. The messenger fell into the river and was killed. The crows on his shoulders flapped off calling angrily: "Caw! Caw! Caw!"

The prince shook his head. "Again! You knew what was going to happen. How?"

Basil said: "I saw it in a dream."

The prince looked at him doubtfully. "Well, however it was, I am grateful. You shall be my body-servant forever."

Together they rode on to the king's palace. Both the king and the queen seemed surprised to see the prince. Basil decided that Queen Epiria was very beautiful. But sitting on her shoulders were two pet black crows.

For a year they all lived happily in the palace.

Then the prince fell in love with the princess of a nearby kingdom. He decided to marry her. Queen Epiria gave him a beautiful carriage—all red and gold paint, with fine leather cushions. "Bring the princess here for the wedding," the king directed.

The prince told Basil, "Protect her for me," and sent him off in the carriage to the princess' palace. She was every bit as lovely as the prince had said.

But as they were riding back, Basil noticed a peculiar thing. Sitting on the driver's shoulders were two black crows. He heard them say:

"Caw. When the carriage reaches the top of the next hill, the driver will jump off. A raging wind will whirl the carriage up into the clouds. When the wind stops, the carriage will fall back to earth. Everyone in it will be killed. Caw, caw. We know, but if any human tells what we have said, he will turn to stone from his waist to the top of his head."

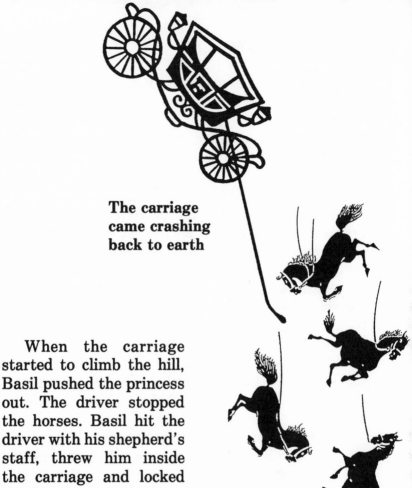

**The carriage
came crashing
back to earth**

When the carriage started to climb the hill, Basil pushed the princess out. The driver stopped the horses. Basil hit the driver with his shepherd's staff, threw him inside the carriage and locked the door.

Then Basil leaped into the driver's seat, snapped the whip above the horses, and drove the carriage up the hill. Just before it reached the top, Basil jumped to safety.

A great wind lifted the carriage up into the clouds. After a moment, the wind stopped and the carriage fell back to earth. It smashed to pieces. All that could be seen were two crows flapping off crying angrily: "Caw, caw, caw."

Basil and the princess walked onward to the king's palace. When they came into the throne room, both the king and the queen were very surprised. The queen asked: "Why are you on foot? Where is the carriage I gave you?"

Basil said: "I am sorry, your highness, but it was destroyed in an accident."

Later the prince asked him: "What happened? Another—dream?"

Basil smiled. "Another dream."

"Humph," said the prince. Then: "I wonder. I wonder if they will ever let me become king."

The next day, Basil was summoned before the royal throne. The king was there, looking very fierce, and the queen, with the two crows back on her shoulders.

The queen pointed at Basil and said: "That shepherd is evil. He must be killed."

And without giving Basil a chance to answer, the king said to his guards: "Guilty. There is a gallows in the courtyard. Take him out and hang him."

The prince protested. But the king told him: "Be quiet! You will not be king here until you marry and have a son. I am still this kingdom's ruler. And I say—Guards, hang him. Now!"

They dragged Basil off to the gallows. As they were putting the rope around his neck, he shouted to the crowd: "Let me tell you what really happened!"

Then he told them quickly how the messenger had tried to kill the prince at the bridge. At that, one of the crows on the queen's shoulder said "Caw!" Basil turned to stone from his toes to his waist.

Then Basil shouted out about the queen's carriage and how the princess had almost been killed. The crow on the queen's other shoulder said

"Caw!" and Basil turned to stone from his waist to the top of his head.

The king shouted: "Stop his lies! Hang him!"

The soldiers pulled on the rope.

But by now Basil's whole body, including his neck, was stone. And do you think a rope can choke the breath out of a stone man?

No, they couldn't kill Basil by hanging.

The king jerked out his sword and aimed a mighty slash at Basil's stone body. The sword blade broke into a hundred pieces.

The king couldn't figure any way to kill this stone man. So he shouted to the guards: "Take him away. Lock him in the dungeon." And they did.

The prince and princess went back to their rooms, very sad at seeing their dearest friend turned to stone for having helped them.

That night the two crows came and perched on the window of Basil's dungeon. They said: "Caw. We have turned this enemy to stone. The prince and the princess die next. The king and queen will give them, for their wedding, two beautiful robes. But whoever puts on these robes will be burned to ashes."

Just imagine the terrible fix Basil was in. How could he warn the prince and princess not to put on those robes? He couldn't talk. He couldn't even move his stone lips. Or blink his stone eyes.

He thought. Very, very hard. Until his brain ached.

And upstairs in the palace, the prince suddenly sat up in his bed. He was shivering. "I just had a bad dream," he said, "a terrible nightmare. In my mind, someone was telling me . . . Yes! It was Basil!

I saw what must be done to free him from the enchantment!"

The prince put on his slippers. Very silently—it was night and everyone else was asleep—he crept into Queen Epiria's bedroom. Beside her bed, on their perch, her two crows were sleeping.

The prince crept up to them and seized each one around the neck, so it couldn't let out a single "Caw." He squeezed and squeezed until they were dead.

The prince crept out of the queen's bedroom and down to the palace kitchen. With a hatchet, the prince cut off the crows' heads.

He drained their blood into a bowl. Then he took the bowl down to the dungeon. Reaching through the bars, he rubbed the crows' blood all over the stone man.

The enchantment was broken. Feeling came back into Basil's arms and legs. He sat up and said: "Thank you, my prince."

The prince told him: "Sssh! Here is the key to your dungeon. The guard was asleep, so I stole it from him. You can let yourself out, run to the woods and hide."

But Basil said: "No. I will not hide! The king and queen are planning to kill you. Tomorrow, at your wedding." And he told the prince exactly what to do.

The next day, the royal wedding of the prince and princess took place. Afterwards, the queen and king held up beautiful robes of bright red satin. Queen Epiria gave them to the prince, saying very sweetly: "Here, try these on. They should keep you . . . warm."

Just then there was a terrible crash. The door into the throne room burst open.

There stood Basil, carrying his staff. He began moving forward very stiffly, as if he were still made of stone.

A soldier ran toward him. Basil knocked him down with his staff.

All the people, including the king and queen, were staring. "The man of stone!" they murmured. "How can anyone fight a man of stone?"

Basil pointed his staff at the king and queen. "I have come to put an end to your treachery," he warned. Everyone in the hall stood watching him.

The prince slipped around behind the king and queen. He opened the two red robes that Queen Epiria had given him. He threw them, one over the king and one over the queen.

Instantly, the cloaks filled with fire. The flames shot up out of the collars, around the heads of the king and queen. More fire poured out of the ends of the robes' sleeves.

The king and queen crumpled to the floor. In a minute, where each of them had stood, there was only a pile of smoking white ashes.

The prince turned to the people and said: "You see what the king and queen tried to do to me and my new bride. They deserved their fate."

The prince and princess were crowned king and queen on the spot. They lived happily ever after.

And Basil? He was made chief of the kingdom's forests and lands. And he was a good chief. Because he, better than any other man, knew what was really meant by the twittering of the birds, and the bark of foxes, and the squeaking of field mice.

Behind that wall of thorns she slept,

Princess

Long ago there lived a king and a queen who were no longer young. Each day they told each other: "If only we had a child." But they had none.

One afternoon the Queen was walking in the gentle woods behind the palace. Beside a deep pool of water, she knelt and wept silently.

Presently a Frog hopped out of the water beside her. He croaked: "Beautiful queen, we know how your heart longs for a child. Follow me."

Down into the pool he swam, so deep the water changed from bright blue to dark grey. After him swam the Queen. As she approached the muddy bottom, she could see him sitting beside a stone that glowed red as blood. The Frog beckoned, and she touched it. A tingling shot up her arm.

enchanted, for a hundred years . . .

Briar Rose

Then, her lungs bursting, she let herself float up to the surface of the water. She crawled out on the bank and the Frog followed her.

As the Queen caught her breath, the Frog said: "Your wish will be fulfilled. Soon you will bring a child into the world."

But the Queen did not believe him.

She could see that the sun was setting, and said: "I must go home to my husband, the King. Thank you, kind Frog, and goodbye."

The Frog called after her: "Do not thank me! Thank my Mistress Of The Red Cloak!" But the Queen did not hear.

Yet everything happened just as the Frog had foretold. The Queen did give birth to a child, a beautiful baby girl. So overjoyed was the King that he ordered a great christening feast prepared. To it he invited everyone of importance. Especially the Twelve Fairies who year-round stand guard over the kingdom.

The day of the feast, the Fairies came down from the sky in a great white boat covered with swan's feathers. When they got out, one by one, their garments sparkled as if woven from starlight and moonbeams.

The King and Queen, bowing, seated them at the table of honor. Behind flowers, on the white linen tablecloth, were spaced twelve great golden plates marked January, February, March, and so on . . . one plate for each month of the year, one plate for each fairy.

When the meal was finished, the Fairies gathered around the child's crib to present their gifts. The first gave the little girl virtue, the second beauty, the third modesty, the fourth riches . . . Until, by the eleventh gift, the child had received all a mother could wish for.

Suddenly the doors of the hall were flung open with a crash. In the sweep of wind, all the candles went out. In the firelight that remained, a Frog could be seen hopping up the carpet.

The Frog was followed by a woman in a great red cloak with a hood hiding her face. She stopped before the Queen, thrust out empty hands, and screamed: "Why did you not invite me, who *gave you* the child?"

The King drew his sword and held it over the crib. But the woman in the red cloak laughed: "Aaahahaha. I too bring a gift." Pointing with a crooked finger at the crib, she said in a voice that

began as a whisper and ended in a shriek:

> *"At childhood's end, in her thirteenth year,*
> *A needle sharp shall prick her here*
> *And she shall die, your daughter dear.*
> *You cannot save her. Wait in fear."*

She swept the red cloak in front of her face and backed, slowly, from the hall.

When the doors had closed on her, the candles magically relighted themselves. Everyone was overcome with terror. The Queen knelt weeping beside the child's crib. The King dropped his sword on the stone floor and bowed his head.

Then the Twelfth Fairy came forward. She said: "My gift I give now.

> *"I cannot lift this dreadful curse,*
> *But we can soften it with our tears.*
> *She shall not die, but rather sleep,*
> *In safety held, for a hundred years."*

And from her dress she took a rose which she placed on the child's crib. And from that day onward, the child was known as Princess Briar Rose.

The next day, the King ordered all needles and pins and other sharp objects taken out of the palace and any place for five miles around. But do you think that was enough to protect the princess from the curse?

As the little girl grew, all of the gifts the fairies had brought her came true. So beautiful was she, and kind, and modest, that all who knew her could not but love her. And she learned everything a princess should know, except how to embroider—because, of course, she was never allowed near anything sharp like a needle.

Now, the rose that the Twelfth Fairy had given her did not die. The royal gardener planted it outside the palace. There it grew into a splendid bush. But all year round it remained green. On only one day during the year—on the princess' birthday —did it burst into blossom, pink, and white, and yellow.

And thus the years passed.

When the girl's thirteenth birthday came near, the King and Queen ordered a great birthday party for her. Everyone in the palace was getting ready, cooking and baking and wrapping presents and stringing colored streamers. Nobody was paying any attention to the princess.

So off she wandered to a part of the palace where she had never been before. There the stone was very old and grey, covered with green moss. Set in the wall was a dark winding staircase. As Princess Briar Rose climbed, she had to brush the cobwebs out of her way, and she was startled when a mouse scurried across the steps in front of her sandals.

At the top of the steps was a small door, very

old, with a curved top and a rusty key in the lock. She turned the key and went in.

On a wooden bench sat an old woman in a red cloak, her hands moving over the filmy white cloth in her lap.

Briar Rose curtseyed. "Good day, granny. What are you doing?"

"I am sewing, my dear. And this—this is a wedding dress." The old woman's hands stopped, and she looked up slyly. "Would you like to try it on?"

What thirteen-year-old girl could resist that?

But when she'd put on the gown, she said in disappointment: "Oh, I'm tall enough. But it's too big here . . . and here . . . "

The old woman told her: "That's all right, I'll just pin up the hem. Hold my needle and thread for me—here!"

Of course, as soon as Briar Rose touched the needle, it pricked her finger. She watched in horror as the drop of blood formed on her fingertip.

Then she began to feel faint. The old woman helped her lie back on the bench. And as Briar Rose fell asleep, throughout the palace, all movement stopped.

The woman in the kitchen, beating the batter for the birthday cake, froze with her elbow in the air. The boy dumping logs on the cooking fire became a kneeling statue; the meat ceased turning on the spit, and the fire died. The girl setting the party table paused as she reached out a match to light the candles. Upstairs in her dressing room, the Queen became motionless as she raised her lipstick before the mirror. The King, who was putting on his trousers, halted with one knee high in the air.

Outside in the courtyard, the dogs stopped chasing their tails and lay down in the dust. The flies settled on the walls; their buzzing faded away. The breeze died. The leaves fell silent. On the roof, the banner on the flagstaff hung limp.

And the palace . . . slept.

But outside, the rosebush that had been the fairy's gift began to change. The petals of the beautiful flowers fell one by one. And then the bush began to grow. New roots began to crawl across the dirt. They sent up thick twisting branches covered with sharp thorns. And still the bush spread, until it had formed a protecting circle around the entire palace. The tough green wall of branches and leaves and thorns grew higher . . . and higher . . . until only the roof of the palace could be seen. Then even the roof, and the flagpole, were hidden.

As the years passed, princes came to try to force their way through that wall of green. But the tough branches wound around them, and the thorns stabbed at them, until they hung still and quiet.

In the village nearby, the story was told of the beautiful Princess Briar Rose asleep with all of her court behind the magic wall of green. Mothers told the tale to their children, who grew up and became parents and told it to their children, who grew up and told it to their children. Until so many years had passed that no one was sure if it was really true or just a legend.

After many many more years, another prince came. A very old man told him of the sleeping princess. The prince said: "I have searched over all the earth and I have not found happiness. I would look on the face of this beautiful sleeping princess."

The next day the prince returned with his sword, to try to cut a way through the thorn bushes. But the hundred years had passed. To his amazement, the green bushes were covered with blossoms—pink, and white, and yellow.

An opening appeared in the bushes before him, and when he had passed in, the bushes closed behind him.

The prince marvelled as he walked slowly by all the sleeping figures. At last he came to the winding staircase and climbed it. Inside, on the bench, he found Princess Briar Rose lying pale as death.

But the drop of blood on her finger was still bright red, for it had never dried. He took his handkerchief and wiped it off. And as he did, the color came back into her cheeks, and she began to breathe again.

So beautiful was she that he leaned forward and kissed her. As their lips met, she opened her eyes and looked on him with love.

Then he raised her up and they could see that the dress, for which she had once been too small, she now filled out beautifully.

She led the prince back through the palace. As she touched each sleeping figure on the forehead, it came awake and began to do again what it had been doing a hundred years before. The woman in the kitchen resumed beating the cake batter. The boy tossed the rest of the logs on the fire and the blaze leaped up; the meat began to sizzle and turn again on the spit. The girl at the party table finished lighting the candles. In the dressing room, the King lowered his leg into his trousers—and wondered why he felt so tired.

Outside, the wind began to blow again. The

leaves rustled; the doves took their heads from under their wings and flew off. On the roof, the flag snapped up.

There sounded a fanfare of trumpets. Church bells pealed from the cathedral nearby, and a golden carriage approached to take the prince and Briar Rose to their wedding. Afterward, in the palace, a party was held, and what had been intended so long ago as birthday gifts became wedding presents instead.

In that beautiful old palace, the prince and Princess Briar Rose lived on in perfect happiness. And when they were blessed with children, to provide a place for them to play, they planted behind the palace a great garden where the bushes bloom pink and white and yellow. But in all that garden they planted only one kind of flower—can you guess what kind it was?

Yes, roses.

So now, the next time you touch a rose, or smell one, think of Princess Briar Rose and her prince. And of the palace—for if they have not died, they live there still.

THE CREEPING SKULLS

About five years ago I was on a walking tour through England. Just as it was getting dark, I reached Lidwell Abbey. Now, an abbey is a group of buildings where holy monks live and pray. But I could see that this abbey had not been in use for hundreds of years. The roofs had caved in. The stained glass had fallen out of all the arched windows. The crumbling stone walls were almost hidden behind ancient moss and long green ivy. Even the stone fences had been beaten down, by the wind and rain, into long rough piles of rubble.

Then I thought I saw, high up in one of the empty windows, the figure of a monk in his black robe and hood. He was placing what looked like a lighted candle in the window.

I knew something odd was going on, because no one was supposed to be living in those deserted ruins any more. So I went into the courtyard in the center of the buildings for a closer look. Shining through the window opening was a freshly-risen star. I said to myself: "You dope. Think you're seeing a ghost's candle and it's just a simple star."

Later that night, in the pub, I laughed and told them what had happened. They didn't laugh. The pub owner asked me to describe the dark figure. Then he nodded his head soberly and said: "Aye, ye ha' seen the ghost of Lidwell Abbey." And he told me how the ghost had come to be.

Our story begins more than three hundred years ago, in the Year Of Our Lord 1671. Even at that time, Lidwell Abbey was almost empty, although its buildings were still in good repair. Only one man lived there, wearing the black robe and hood of a monk. At night, he would place a single lighted candle in a window as a welcome to passing travelers.

But few travelers came that way. Because Lidwell Abbey stands far out in the country, along a little-used road. However—

One night black with clouds, a traveler did come by. He was about 40, powerfully muscled, and bow-legged from many years at sea. On his back he carried a long pack wrapped in oilskins. It was just beginning to rain when he saw the candle.

He knocked at the refectory's great oaken door.

Slowly the door opened a crack. Inside he could see a short heavyset man in black, a hood shadowing his face. "What seek ye?"

"Shelter. Against the rain and the night."

Opening the door, the man in black smiled and gestured. "Enter and be . . . blessed."

The man in black led him to a long table. The

sailor was amazed to see it set with a great stand of beef, roast potatoes, cheese, apples, a loaf of heavy black bread, and red wine. The sailor commented: "For a monk, you live well."

The man in black said: "God provides."

The sailor's gaze roved around the deserted dining hall. Its white walls were decorated with jeweled daggers, silver drinking cups, sparkling necklaces and musical instruments. "Strange decorations," the sailor mused, "for a House Of God."

The man in black shrugged. "Gifts. Left by travelers who . . . who decided to stay the night."

The monk was eyeing the oilskin pack. The hood had fallen back from his dark face. In the candlelight, the sailor could see the bloodshot eyes, the heavy cheeks covered with short beard. "Perhaps," suggested the monk, "you would like to add a gift?"

The sailor said: "No. I have nothing to offer as valuable as the things you already have."

The man in black bowed his head and said: "As God wills it." But his fingers crept along the worn tabletop and began to probe greedily at the oilskin pack.

As the night wore on, the wine began to warm the sailor's blood. He spoke happily of his years along the Spanish Main. Of sea battles and boardings, and men put to the plank.

At that, the monk leaped up and pointed an accusing finger. "You have been a pirate! It is the devil's work you have been doing. If you are to save yourself from hell's fire, you must be baptized, confess, and be shriven!"

The sailor felt, now that he was on land, perhaps he should lead a holier life. He agreed.

The man in black said: "I will baptize you myself. Now! Follow me to the chapel."

The sailor started to pick up his oilskin pack. The man in black said sharply: "Leave it. You will not need it. Not where *you* are going."

They made their way through the darkness, across the courtyard and past its deep well.

In the tiny chapel, the man in black placed his candle in a holder on the wall. It shone down on a wide stone baptismal font with a shallow depression in its middle.

"Kneel!" he commanded, motioning. "Place your head on the rim of the stone. Close your eyes. And say farewell to your sinful life!"

The sailor placed his forehead against the cold stone. But he felt uneasy at the darkness and the quiet. Then he remembered. In the baptismal font, there had been no water. How could the man in black baptize him without holy water?

The sailor opened his eyes and looked up. Just in time to see the man in black, his eyes glaring, lifting high a heavy brass candlestick.

The sailor rolled aside just as the candlestick smashed down where his head had been.

The sailor leaped up. "You are no true monk! You are a robber disguised in monk's clothing!"

They fought. But the sailor was very strong. He threw the monk down on the stone floor. "It was my pack you wanted! Now I know how you got all those rich 'presents' on your walls. How many other travelers have you killed? And where did you throw their bodies?"

The man in black snarled: "I will tell you nothing."

The sailor said: "You will hang. I will take you into the village, to the judge."

The man in the black robe sneered: "How? I will not go willingly. And you—you do not have the strength to drag me all that way."

The sailor thought: That is true, it is a long way. Where can I imprison him while I bring the judge here?

Then the sailor remembered the deep well outside in the courtyard. Its bottom was dry, covered with something white. It had smooth walls. If the robber were put down, he could not climb out.

The sailor dragged the robber into the courtyard. But when the robber saw where the sailor was going to put him, he screamed: "No! Anywhere else! But not down there! You do not know what . . . what waits for me . . . down there."

The sailor mocked: "Waits? Nothing waits! It is your conscience that waits." And he thrust him down into the well.

As the sailor made his way off toward the village, behind him, from the well, he could hear the robber's tortured screaming.

Hours later, the sailor returned with the judge, and soldiers carrying a hangman's noose. But as they approached the well, all was silence. The screaming had stopped.

The judge shined his lantern down the well. On its bottom could be seen the robber's body, lying on something white. The black robe was soggy with blood.

A soldier was lowered down into the well. The rope was tied around the robber's body, under the armpits, and he was lifted up. When he was at eye level, they could see that the robber's face and body had been ripped open and torn, as if by the teeth of wild animals.

The judge shook his head. "A horrible death. But deserved."

"Yes," said the sailor. "But down there, in that empty well, what killed him?"

Just then came a cry from the soldier. He began to hand up the white things covering the bottom of the well. They were bones—arm bones, leg bones, ribs, spines.

The sailor shuddered. "Now we know where he threw the bodies of the travelers he killed. How those bones must have wished that some time they could be revenged."

The judge asked: "Yes. But down there in the well, lying on those bones, what tore his body to pieces? What killed him?"

Then came another cry from the soldier at the bottom of the well. He began handing up the skulls of the murdered travelers.

They were placed in a row along the top of the stone fence. Looking at them, you could see the black eye sockets . . . the empty spaces where the noses had been . . .

Underneath each skull hung a powerful jawbone. The jaws were filled with sharp teeth.

And all those teeth were dripping fresh blood.

Woodcut by Leslie Ferrara

IN Southwest China lived a very old woman. She had a grown son. One afternoon he foolishly went walking alone in the hills.

A tiger ate him.

The old woman cried and cried. Then she limped to the village court. She pointed her finger at the judge. "You are in charge of bringing justice. Punish the tiger."

The judge smiled. "We leave that to the hunters. Policemen do not arrest tigers and bring them into court."

Beating her chest, the old woman cried out: "That tiger killed my son. He is a murderer. I demand justice!"

The judge scratched his chin. "Old woman, don't be unreasonable. I can do nothing. Go to the temple. Pray for your son."

The old woman fell to her knees, wailing: "I am old enough to be *your* mother. Do you not honor your own ancestors? Then have some respect for my age."

Now, they try in China to be very kind to old people. And the judge was a good man at heart. So he said: "Look, I will do what I can. I will issue an order to my policemen—an order to try to arrest the tiger."

The old woman watched him write out the order. Then she went home.

The judge called in his policemen. "I have an order here to arrest a tiger," he said, holding it out. "Which one of you will do it?"

Now, one of the policemen—named Ho Ning— had been drinking wine. He was very drunk, but he didn't want the judge to know. So he pretended to be very brave instead. He gave a big salute and said: "I will carry out that order. I, Ho Ning, will arrest the villain. For I fear neither man nor beast."

He took the order and staggered home. The next morning he woke up with a headache. And when he read who he had agreed to arrest—do you think he was so brave then?

He went back to the judge and said: "You—you were just kidding, weren't you?"

The judge told him sternly: "That woman is old enough to be your mother too. Have some respect for her grey hairs. Anyhow, you offered. Now go and DO IT!"

So Ho Ning went off into the jungle. But he didn't hunt for the tiger. He just hid behind trees.

After a couple of days, he came back to the judge and said: "I swear I searched everywhere for that tiger. But I just couldn't find him. He must have

THE FAITHFUL TIGER

heard me coming. I'm sure he was so afraid of me he ran away and hid somewhere."

If you had been the judge, would you have believed a story like that?

The judge had the other policemen beat Ho Ning with bamboo rods on the bottoms of his bare feet, and oh! how that hurt. Then the judge put the tip of his nose against the tip of Ho Ning's nose and shouted: "Now go back and find him!"

Well, back Ho Ning had to go into the jungle. He kept looking over his shoulder. And whistling very loudly to warn the tiger away.

Finally his wanderings brought him to a great deserted temple. Inside, at the far end, rose a big stone statue of Buddha. He went before it and knelt, praying for safety.

Just then there sounded a growl. In through the temple door came the tiger.

Ho Ning fell flat on the floor. He prayed the tiger hadn't seen him. Or wasn't hungry.

The tiger lay down near the doorway and began to lick his paws.

Finally Ho Ning got his courage back. He stood up and moved sideways toward the tiger. In one hand he had a rope. With the other hand, he held out the judge's order—as if the tiger could read it!

Trying to sound very brave, he said: "T-T-T-Tiger, you're under arrest. B-B-By order of the judge." The tiger growled a little, and Ho Ning leaped back. "Now, don't be angry with me. I'm just doing my duty. If you have to eat somebody, eat the judge. He wrote the order."

The tiger licked his teeth. Ho Ning edged forward again. "Anyhow, if you are the tiger who killed that old woman's son, you've caused a lot of trouble for everybody. So just put your head down and let me slip this rope around your neck."

Well, you know, it really was the tiger who ate the old woman's son. And there in the temple, the tiger did put his head down and let Ho Ning tie the rope around it.

Then Ho Ning led the tiger through the village. And into the judge's court.

When the judge saw who was at the other end of Ho Ning's rope, he gave out a yell and hid behind his desk.

But when the tiger didn't eat anybody—right away—the judge looked with one eye around the

Illustration by
Carol Jenkins

side of his desk and asked: "Was it you who ate that old woman's son?"

The tiger nodded his head.

The judge slowly stood up. He began reading in one of his thick lawbooks, following the words with his finger. Finally he said: "Well, that makes you a murderer. The law says—let me see here—the law says the punishment for murderers is death."

At that the tiger bared his long pointed teeth and let out a roar, as if he were going to eat everything in the courtroom—the judge, the policemen, even the flowers on the judge's desk.

The judge dived down behind his desk again. Without putting his head up, he added quickly: "No, no, not you, of course. The law does not even mention tigers. Oh, this is a very difficult case."

The judge stood up again and straightened his robes, saying: "I have to be just to the old woman, you understand. She's old enough to be my own mother. She's much too old to work. When you killed her son, you took away the only person who was taking care of her . . .

"Tiger! Why don't **you** promise to take care of her? Just as if she were your own mother! Then I can write in my lawbook that justice has been done."

The tiger nodded and padded out of the courtroom. And the next morning, when the old woman opened the door of her cottage, to her great surprise, there lay a freshly-killed deer.

The old woman cut off the deer's hide to make warmer clothing for herself. She kept some of the deer's flesh to cook a rich stew. The rest she sold to buy rice. And that night she enjoyed the best dinner she'd eaten in years.

From then on, every morning the tiger brought

her something. Sometimes it was an animal's body. But when the tiger killed a hunter, or a rich merchant walking through the hills, the tiger would be sure to bring the old woman his purse full of money and jewels.

Robbers never bothered the old woman. You see, at night the tiger would sleep on her porch, right in front of the door. And do you think any robbers were foolish enough to try to sneak in by stepping over him?

After some years, the old woman died. All her nieces and nephews came to mourn her. Even the judge came from the emperor's palace. By now he was very famous—the only judge in China who had ever punished a tiger in court.

They buried the old woman in a field full of flowers. Just as they were putting the last shovelful of dirt on the grave, the tiger came trotting out of the jungle. Everyone ran away except the judge, who nodded at his old friend.

The tiger put his front paws on the grave and let out a roar—AHHRRR! Then he turned and trotted back into the jungle, and was never seen again.

The judge returned to the emperor's palace and told what had happened.

The old emperor was so impressed that he had a place to pray built over the old woman's grave. Above the entrance the emperor had a sign placed reading: "The Shrine Of The Faithful Tiger."

And there it remains to this day.

The Seven Ravens

There once lived a king who dressed all in black, and in a neighboring country, a king who dressed all in green.

To the Black King and his wife were born seven children. But one after the other, they were all boys.

When the queen announced she was expecting her eighth child, the king told her: "All my life I have longed for a daughter." His face grew fierce. "If this child be a girl, the seven boys shall die, so she may inherit the entire kingdom."

Then he had seven white coffins built. He filled them with wood shavings, and in each he placed a plump death pillow, embroidered with the name of one of the sons.

The queen wept. Her youngest son Benjamin, who was lame, asked: "Mother, why do you cry?"

She touched his hair. "Because I do not wish you or any of my children to die." Then she showed him the seven waiting coffins.

Benjamin wiped her tears. "We will run away and save ourselves."

She commanded: "Hide deep in the forest. There keep watch from the highest tree. After the child is born, I will have a banner flown from the castle tower. If this be another boy, the banner will be white. Then you will know it is safe to return home. But if the child be a girl"—the queen choked back a sob—"the banner will be red. Then you will know you must flee to the country of the Green King. And I will pray to heaven to protect you from the Green King's evil mother."

The queen summoned her seven sons. They formed a line before her. With trembling hands, she marked crosses in the air over their heads, blessing them. Then, one by one, they made their way off into the forest. Some carried bows, and some spears, so their father the king would think they were simply going hunting.

Day after day, from the treetops, they kept watch. On the seventh day, the child was born. The brothers held their breaths as the banner at the top of the tower slowly uncurled in the wind.

The banner was blood red.

The brothers thought of the waiting coffins.

In silence the brothers made their way across the border into the country of the Green King. Deep in his forest, they built for themselves a fine white house. Around it ran a low green hedge, covered with tiny white star-shaped flowers, of a plant named "starwort." There they lived by hunting and fishing. Lame Benjamin remained at home, cooking the trout and quail and deer they brought back each night.

Thus passed twelve years. The little girl, in the castle of the king who dressed in black, grew into a beautiful young woman. But on her forehead shone a strange birthmark—a star shape that, when she became excited, glowed silver.

On her thirteenth birthday, she wandered into a part of the castle where she had not been before. She found the seven empty bedrooms. When she asked to whom they belonged, her mother told her for the first time of her brothers.

The girl clapped her hands in delight. "Brothers! Oh, mother, I must find them."

Sadly her mother blessed her, and she set out. She searched first through the country of her father, the king who dressed in black. But, of course, she could not find them there. Then on she went into the country of the Green King. There she made her way softly and silently, for she too had heard that the Green King's mother was cruel and evil, with witches as friends.

Presently the girl came upon a fine white house surrounded by a hedge covered with tiny white star-shaped flowers. From behind the hedge rose a lame young man. He marveled at her royal garments and the star on her forehead. "Whom do you seek?" he asked.

She said: "My seven princely brothers, whom I have never seen."

He gestured at the house and told her: "You are at home."

That night, when the six brothers returned from their day's hunting, they laughed and cried and were happy together.

The next morning she told them: "I would stay here with you, instead of returning to our father the king." And from that day on, Benjamin could join his brothers hunting. Each evening, when they returned, she would have a delicious dinner waiting.

Thus passed a year, a happy year. At its end, thinking to have a celebration, she picked all of the white star-shaped flowers from the hedge. Some she placed as garlands around the dinner plates. The others she used to decorate the house.

But when the brothers came home that night, their faces turned white with fear. "Do you know what you have done?" they cried out. "You have destroyed us! Those white flowers were our only protection against the magic of the Green King's evil mother. When dawn comes, her curse will fall upon us."

"I did not know! How can I save you? There must be a way."

The brothers answered: "Yes, but it would be difficult. For seven years you must remain absolutely silent, speaking no word nor laughing. During those years you must spin starwort into thread, and from it make for us seven white robes with stars on their breasts. Do that, and we will be released."

She bowed her head. "I will try."

They resolved to take what last pleasure they could. They ate the roast venison she had prepared, and drank the wine they had been saving. They played their musical instruments. But sadness crept into their songs as the dawn approached.

The seven brothers stood before the house. Speeding from the horizon, the first beam of sunlight touched them. Their backs began to bend. Feathers formed on their arms. Their noses lengthened into beaks. Slowly they changed into seven black ravens. With mournful cries, they lunged forward and flew up into the sky.

At that same moment, the house and the hedge vanished. The girl found herself alone in the forest. She wondered if, to save her brothers, she would have the strength to remain silent for seven years.

She filled her apron with starwort and climbed

into a tree, where she would be safe from wild animals. And there, under her nimble fingers, the robe of a royal prince began to take shape.

Thus passed four years—silent years, because even when the needle pricked her finger, she dare not let herself cry out. During those four years, four of the robes were completed.

As the fifth year began, the youthful Green King, hunting alone, came riding through the forest. He found his hunting dogs surrounding a giant oak tree, barking madly at a slight white figure high in its branches. Not knowing if it were man or beast, he called up: "Holla, what are you?"

When no answer came, he cocked his crossbow, fitted a bolt, and raised the weapon. But before he could shoot, a golden bracelet dropped from the tree to his feet.

He lowered the crossbow. Looking more closely, he now could see that it was a beautiful young woman. Although her white gown was in rags, she bore herself with the dignity of a princess. He asked again: "Who are you?"

When no answer came, he thought: "This is the strangest maiden I have even seen." He climbed the tree and gently brought her down. When he saw how torn her dress was, he drew his own green cloak around her shoulders. Taking her before him on his horse, he rode with her back to his palace.

There he had her dressed in rich garments. From all the surrounding countries he summoned wise men to talk to her in their native languages. But to no word did she reply. The only sound that came from her was the clicking of her knitting needles.

In the days that followed, the Green King had her sit beside him at table. So courteous and modest and kind was she that he began to think: "In all the world, this is the one woman I wish as my queen."

So they were wed, in a ceremony of great magnificence. Yet when it came time to speak the vows of marriage, she simply nodded. And the people of the countryside marveled, calling her "The Silent Queen."

Thus passed her fifth year. During it, the fifth of the robes was completed. At year's end, a child was born to them. The king presented it to her, asking: "What name do you wish to give our son?"

She had to choke back her answer.

At that the king's evil mother leaped forward screaming: "Aahahaha! You see! She cares naught for the child. She cares for nothing but those robes at which she knits without stop." The old woman hunched over, cocked her head to one side, and suggested: "Is she perhaps knitting a spell?"

"No!" protested the king. "She is too pious and good to do anything of that kind."

The mother sneered: "Who knows from whence she comes?" Off she hobbled, muttering: "She is not worthy of a king—no, not of **you**, my fine son."

That night the king's evil mother crept into the royal bedroom and stole away the child. She gave it to the soldiers. Then she returned and shook the king awake, saying: "My son, this woman you have married is nothing but a common murderer. For behold, the crib is empty! She has killed your child and hidden its body."

The king sobbed: "No, no, no, no. Wife, defend yourself! Tell us that you are innocent!"

But the only sound that came from her was the clicking of the knitting needles . . .

The sixth year went by. Much of the time she spent on the roof of the palace, knitting. Each morning the seven ravens would fly overhead with mournful cries. Looking up, she would whisper: "If only once I could cry out to you. If only once I could say 'Have faith in me!' "

But she dared not speak a single word aloud. Faster and faster flew her needles. By year's end, the sixth of the robes was completed.

A second child was born to her and the Green King. Again, at night, the evil mother stole the boy away. Then she waked the king, telling him: "Behold! Once again the crib is empty. Once again she has killed the child and hidden its body. Have you not yet discovered what she is? That great star that shines on her forehead—is that not the *sign* of witchcraft?"

The king demanded: "Wife! Tell me that you did not do this terrible thing. Speak!"

But the only sound that came was the click-click click-click of the knitting needles.

And the king began to doubt.

The seventh year went by. The seventh robe was almost finished, except for a missing sleeve. A third child was born to the Silent Queen. Once more the Green King's mother stole away the child.

But this time, not satisfied, she returned to the royal bedroom. With a needle she pricked her own fingertip. Carefully she smeared the blood on the lips of the sleeping queen.

Then she roused the Green King, hissing: "How much more proof do you need? Look at her mouth! This time she has not only killed the child—she has eaten its body!"

The king pleaded: "Wife, wife. If ... if you are innocent, you must speak now."

But her lips remained still. Only her knitting

"Who are you knitting those robes for? Speak!"

needles moved—click-click, click-click, click-click.

The king's mother shouted triumphantly: "Her very silence condemns her!"

The king said sadly: "It must be true. It must be that my mother is right. You *are* a murderer. My duty is clear. Tomorrow, at dawn, you must be burned at the stake."

The queen gasped. Because she knew that her seven years of silence would not be over until the sun rose that morning.

All that night she knelt on the stone floor of the palace dungeon, praying and knitting. By now the seventh robe was complete except for the missing sleeve.

Through the window of her cell she could see the black sky growing light in the east.

She laid aside her queen's robes and put on again the torn white dress she had been wearing when the Green King found her in the tree.

The soldiers came for her. She folded the seven robes of starwort over her arm and followed the soldiers to the stake in the public square.

Dry brush was piled about her feet. In the distance she could see the executioner in his black cap approaching, carrying a torch to light the fire that would burn her to death.

Just then the sun rose.

Its first ray of light shot from the horizon and touched her. The great silver star on her forehead began to glow. At the same moment, the seven black ravens flew down out of the sky and landed at her feet.

She threw the robes over the birds.

One by one, as the cloth touched them, they grew taller. They changed back into human form.

Her brothers once more, they drew their swords and formed a circle around their sister.

But over their heads, she cried out in a hoarse voice: "My—my—my husband, the king! At last my seven years of silence are over. The spell is broken. Now I can declare to you my innocence!"

She pointed a trembling finger in accusation. "It is not I who has taken away our children. It is she, your mother—out of fear that by loving us, you would love her less."

The king's mother backed away screaming: "Lies! Lies! All lies! Do not believe her!"

But the soldiers were sent. The three children were found and returned to their parents.

The Green King, tears in his eyes, drew himself up tall and told his mother: "It is not my wife, the once-silent queen, who lies. It is you, my evil mother. And now, the punishment that you arranged for her ... shall be yours instead!"

So the old woman was bound to the stake and burned to ashes.

Thereafter, the Green King and his once-silent queen lived on in the palace in peace and happiness. And in much conversation—because she had seven years of silence to make up for.

The seven brothers lived with them for a time, until they found brides of their own. All who visited the palace said the brothers were each more handsome than the others.

But the most striking of all was the oldest brother, the one who had received the cloak from which one sleeve was missing. For from his left shoulder extended, not an arm ... but the folded black wing of a raven.

THE CREAM WITCH

In Europe there's a country named Switzerland. On its green mountainsides graze herds of cows. From those cows the farmers get rich milk. Some they make into milk chocolate. But much of it they make into cheese. Maybe you've eaten Swiss cheese—it's yellowish white and comes in long slices with lots of round holes in it.

I'm sorry I started you thinking how hungry you are. Let's get back to those mountains. Between them stretch low places called valleys. One is called St. Gotthardt's Pass.

If you walk through St. Gotthardt's Pass today, you'll pass a huge rock. It's big as a house, and white as milk.

Now, that big rock wasn't always there. My grandfather Otto Bradl—he's dead now, God rest his soul—told me how it was in the olden days. Where that rock now rises, there was only a little house.

A woman lived there. She was so old that nobody remembered her real name. The villagers just called her Nidelgret. That means "the cream lady."

The children in the village loved Nidelgret, because she whipped up delicious blueberry shortcake for them. But some parents whispered that Nidelgret must be a witch. You see, she kept only one cow. So she only got one jug of fresh milk each day. But, somehow, she always had more cream than anyone else.

As you can imagine, many of the farmers were jealous of Nidelgret's cream. They kept asking: "Where **does** she get it all?" Finally one farmer decided to find out.

Early one morning, he sneaked into Nidelgret's barn and hid behind a bale of hay.

Well, in came Nidelgret swinging her milk pail. She put the empty pail down in the middle of the barn floor. She took a tiny pitcher of cream and carefully poured the cream into the pail.

Then she reached high into the air and began squeezing each fist together, as if she were milking many cows. Turning to north, then west, then south, then east, she sang in a high voice:

> *"From herdsman's pail,*
> *Pay witch's fee.*
> *From every cow*
> *Two spoonfuls to me!"*

and right out of the air, little jets of cream spurted into her pail until it was full. Then off Nidelgret went with her pailful of cream.

After she'd left, the farmer crept out from behind the bale of hay. He kept muttering the words over and over so he wouldn't forget. You see, he'd figured out that this was a spell. Nidelgret was using it to steal two spoonfuls of cream from every other cow in the village.

At first he was tempted to be honest and tell everybody. Then he thought: "Hunh! Why shouldn't I just help myself? All that cream—I can sell it and be rich!"

So off he went to his own barn. Carefully he closed the big red doors so nobody could spy on him.

He collected all the milkpails he owned. He had to dump a nest of tiny fieldmice out of one of them. In the middle of his barn floor, he lined up all the pails.

He poured a few drops of cream in each pail. Then, slowly turning around, he reached up into the air and began imitating Nidelgret's squeezing motions.

But this farmer was more than dishonest. He was also very greedy. So, instead of asking for two spoonfuls, he roared out:

> *"From herdsman's pail,*
> > *Pay witch's fee.*
> *From every cow*
> > *Two p a i l f u l s to me!"*

No sooner had he said the magic words than cream began to pour out of the air. The great white streams filled all his pails in a minute. They overflowed. The cream rushed over the barn floor and flooded around the farmer's shoes.

He stopped laughing. He was spattered with cream. The entire floor was covered with cream. It rose higher and higher, right up to his knees.

He climbed on a table.

The cream kept pouring out of the air. Soon the table was floating, like a raft on a white ocean. The farmer went down on his hands and knees, to keep from falling off.

"Stop it, stop it!" he shouted.

But had he learned any magic words to stop it?

Up and up the farmer floated. Past the cow stables. Past the hay loft.

"Help! Help! Nidelgret! Make it stop!"

As the farmer's head began bumping the ceiling, he shouted desperately: "Nidelgret! Nidelgret! Make it stop!"

Nidelgret, who lived nearby, heard his cry for help.

When she opened her window, she could see the cream running out under the farmer's barn door, and leaking out around the barn windows.

She knew in an instant what had happened.

She cried out: "You fool! I was content to take a little at a time. But you—you have stolen all the cream in the village for a whole month!"

She put her palms against her cheeks and began to rock unhappily from side to side. "You have spoiled everything. They will never let us go on living in this village."

Her lips pinched tight. She looked up into the sky and whispered: "Let the punishment come."

From the mountains, a great black cloud came boiling through St. Gotthardt's Pass. A terrible windstorm blew away the farmer's barn and Nidelgret's house as if they were dry leaves.

When the storm had passed, the villagers could see that where Nidelgret's house had been, this great white rock now stood. And my grandfather told me—God rest his soul—that it's still there. You can see it when you go walking through St. Gotthardt's Pass.

But there's a strange thing. If you tap the rock with your fingers, it sounds sort of hollow.

The village people will tell you that Nidelgret has the greedy farmer imprisoned inside the rock. There she's keeping watch over him. So he doesn't get into any more mischief, until the Day Of Judgment comes for us all.

THE EMERALD LIZARD

Brother Pedro San Joseph de Bethancourt lived 300 years ago in the city of Santiago in Guatemala. You can still see his tomb there in the chapel of St. Francis.

The robe he wore was simple and shabby; he spent his life caring for the sick and the poor.

In the street one day, a poor Indian approached. Hands clasped before his chest, shoulders hunched, he said: "Padre, my wife is sick—and I have no money for medicine. My little boys cry from hunger—and I have nothing for them to eat."

Brother Pedro said: "God's help is always close by." He felt in the pocket of his robe, but there was not even a stray copper coin. All had been given to the nuns to buy clothing for the poor.

Brother Pedro looked up at the bright sky, waiting. But nothing happened.

At their feet, from a clump of flowers, came a scurrying sound. Into the path ran a small green lizard.

Brother Pedro stooped, caught it, and placed it in the hands of the Indian.

The Indian—his name was Juan Luis—looked at Brother Pedro in bewilderment. Then he looked down at the lizard. What moments before was a living thing had become stiff and lifeless. But still

Illustration by Carol Jenkins

green, green as a jungle fern. And glowing inside, as
if lit by green fire.

The lizard had frozen into priceless emerald.

Juan Luis cried his thanks. Then he ran to a merchant in the marketplace. There he sold the jewel statue for food and medicine.

Years passed. Juan's sons grew up and became important merchants, selling blankets and pottery. Juan himself built a big farm, with fellow-workers and many cattle. Yet he lived simply, saving his money coin by coin.

At last he had enough. He went to the merchant in the market and bought back the emerald lizard. He wrapped it in cloth and set out in search of Brother Pedro.

When Juan found the holy man, he felt sad. Brother Pedro had become old and grey. His clothes were more ragged than ever.

The Indian said: "Greetings to you, Padre. I am Juan Luis. Years ago you gave me an emerald lizard. Now I have brought it back."

He could see Brother Pedro was searching his mind, trying to remember.

Juan Luis opened the cloth and held out the jeweled lizard. It glittered greenly in the sunlight like polished glass.

The Indian pleaded: "Padre, take it. It is yours. It has brought me much good fortune. Now it can make life easy for you. Sell it, and rest from your labors."

Brother Pedro held the statue in his palm. Then, smiling gently, he set it down on the dusty path.

Instantly it turned again into a live lizard. Off it darted, disappearing into the tall grass.

Brother Pedro nodded slightly. Then he slipped his hands deep into his shabby sleeves and turned, making his way down the dusty road toward the church.

From its tower, the small worn bell softly rang the evening prayer—the angelus.

SNOW WHITE

One wintry day, a queen was sewing in her castle tower. When she opened a window to look out, the needle pricked her finger. Three drops of blood fell down to the snow below.

The queen wished: "Would that I had a child with skin white as that snow, and cheeks red as that blood."

Some months later, a daughter was born to the queen. The child did have skin white as snow, and cheeks red as blood. The mother, with her last breath, named the child Snow White. Then the mother died.

A year later, the king married a second time. The new wife was beautiful, but she was also as proud and distant as a leopard. She always wore black—high pointed headdresses and great sweeping cloaks. The servants, and the people of the country, spoke of her in whispers as the Black Queen.

With her she brought to the castle a tall mirror framed in black iron. Alone in her dressing room, she would stand before it and demand:

"Mirror, mirror on the wall . . .
Who is the fairest one of all?"

and the mirror would reply:

"Thou art the fairest in this land."

Then the queen would proudly throw back her long black hair, smile, and do a slow sweeping dance, even though no one else was in the room.

But each day Snow White grew lovelier. And the Black Queen grew older.

On the girl's seventh birthday, the Black Queen asked the looking glass:

"Mirror, mirror on the wall . . .
Who is the fairest one of all?"

and it answered:

"Snow White's now fairest to be seen . . .
Bow to her beauty, stately queen."

The Black Queen's heart filled with jealousy. Her hatred tormented her day and night. Each day she glared at the child.

At last she ordered the royal hunter: "Take the child deep into the forest. Kill her there. But I must have proof that she is dead. Cut out her lungs and liver. Bring them back to me."

The hunter obeyed and took the girl away. Deep in the forest, his eyes filled with tears as he drew his knife.

Snow White pleaded: "Dear huntsman, spare me

my life. I will run deep into this endless forest. Never will I come home again—I promise."

The huntsman said: "I cannot bring myself to kill you. Run away, then." And as she stumbled off, he thought: "Poor child. Soon wild beasts will devour you."

Just then a wild pig came snorting by. Quickly the huntsman killed it. He cut out its lungs and liver. That night he presented them to the queen, saying: "You see? Snow White is dead."

The Black Queen laughed bitterly. She sent the lungs and liver to the kitchen and had them cooked with salt. And for dinner, she ate them.

All night Snow White stumbled through the mysterious forest. The sharp stones cut her feet. Tree branches scratched her face. Overhead, owls hooted. From out of the darkness, she could see the eyes of wild beasts following her.

As the sun rose, Snow White staggered into a meadow. In its center stood a cottage, neat and plain as a loaf of bread. The door was part way open.

Inside the house, Snow White could see a table set with seven little metal plates. On each plate was a little spoon and, beside it, a little drinking mug. Against the wall stood seven little beds. Now, who do you think lived there?

Yes, the dwarfs. They were away, off in a dark

cave, mining copper. But Snow White had fled so far from her own land that she didn't know about them.

Snow White was trembling, she was so hungry and thirsty. She ate some vegetables and bread from each plate, and from each cup she drank a drop of wine. But only one bite and one sip from each, for she did not wish to eat up all of any one person's dinner.

Then she tried out the beds, until she found one that fitted her. There she fell into an exhausted sleep.

That evening she suddenly woke up. Seven candles were shining down on her. Above their flames she could see the stern faces of the dwarfs. "Who are you?" they demanded.

She told them about the jealous Black Queen, and how the huntsman had taken pity on her and let her go.

The dwarfs talked it over. Then they told Snow White: "You may stay with us. All day we work in the mines. If you will take care of our house while we are gone—make the beds, wash, sew, cook, and keep everything neat and clean—you shall want for nothing."

Snow White said: "Yes, I will do it. With all my heart."

So Snow White kept house for the dwarfs and was happy. Each evening, as they came home tired from the mines, she would have supper ready for them, warm and nourishing. And each morning, as they left for the mines, they would shake their fingers at her and warn: "Lock the windows. Bar the door. Let no one in."

Several weeks went by.

One day, back in the castle, the Black Queen stood before the looking glass and asked:

> *"Mirror, mirror on the wall . . .*
> *Who's now the fairest one of all?"*

And the mirror replied:

> *"Snow White grows fairer day by day . . .*
> *She has traveled far away.*
> *Deep within the forest glen*
> *She lives with seven little men."*

The queen's face grew black with rage. She realized that the huntsman had tricked her.

"I will kill the girl myself," she vowed.

Next day, the Black Queen dressed herself as an old peddler woman. She made the long journey through the forest. As she came near the dwarfs' cottage, she smeared dirt on her face as a disguise. Then she knocked on the door, calling out: "Pretty things to sell! Pretty things!"

Snow White opened a second-floor window and leaned out. "It is so long since I have had anything pretty," she thought.

The peddler woman held up a wide, strong belt covered with bright embroidery. "Look! Look! It will make you beautiful as a grown woman. Try it on!"

Slowly, hesitantly, Snow White opened the door and let the peddler woman in.

The woman went behind Snow White, saying: "Dear child, let me help you." She buckled the belt around Snow White's waist. But she pulled it so tight the girl could no longer breathe. She gasped and fell. Gradually the color faded from her cheeks.

The Black Queen threw off her disguise. "Now I am the most beautiful!" she shouted. Over Snow

White's body, she began to spin around in a wild dance of triumph.

When the dwarfs came home that night, they found Snow White lying pale and still. They cut the belt away from her waist. The red came back into Snow White's cheeks. She began to breathe again.

The dwarfs shook their beards and told her: "That peddler woman was really the wicked queen. When we are away, let no one in. No one!"

The next morning, in her castle, the Black Queen stood before the mirror and asked:

> *"Mirror, mirror on the wall . . .*
> *Who's now the fairest one of all?"*

To her amazement, the mirror replied:

> *"Snow White's still fairest to be seen . . .*
> *Bow to her beauty, wicked queen."*

The Black Queen shook with rage. Then her eyes narrowed to slits and she hissed: "Snow White shall die, even if it costs me my own life."

She went to a secret room. There, by spells and witchcraft, she made the most beautiful apple ever seen. But one side she filled with poison.

The next day she disguised herself as a farmer's wife. Back through the forest she made her way, to the dwarfs' cottage.

When she knocked, Snow White called down: "I cannot let anyone in. The dwarfs have forbidden me."

The woman called up: "It's all right, dearie. Let me give you one of my apples. Delicious apples, dearie, to put roses in your cheeks. Oh, don't be afraid. See, I'll cut one in half. Now I'll eat the white half, and you eat the red. Here."

Snow White thought: "The apple must be safe or she would not eat half." So the girl took the red half and bit it. But which half do you think the Black Queen had put the poison in? The half she ate herself—or the half she gave Snow White?

In a moment, Snow White's breathing stopped. She fell dead on the floor beside the window.

Back the Black Queen hurried to her castle. There the magic mirror told her:

"Thou art now fairest to be seen."

And the Black Queen began to dance for joy, spinning about, waving her arms high so her long sleeves billowed out like a raven's wings.

The dwarfs found Snow White on the cottage floor. Nothing they could do would bring her back to life.

Next day they washed her face with water and wine, combed her hair, and dressed her in a new gown. They placed her body on a table in the sun and sat around it crying. Birds came, too, and wept for Snow White—first an owl, then a cardinal, and last a dove.

After three days the dwarfs thought to bury her. But she looked as if she were simply sleeping, her skin white as snow and her cheeks red as blood. They said: "We cannot bear to put her in the cold ground."

So they laid her in a coffin and wrote on its side, in the ancient language the dwarfs use:

Here Lies A King's Daughter

The coffin was made of glass, so you could see Snow White inside.

The coffin was placed on the mountainside where the sun would warm it and the dew moisten it.

Always a dwarf stood by, day and night, guarding it.

Seven years passed.

One day a king's son came hunting alone through the mountains. He read the golden letters written on the glass. He looked in at the calm silent face, and fell in love. Sending his hunting horse back to his home kingdom, he stayed with the dwarfs in their cottage. Each day he helped stand guard beside Snow White's body.

One day a royal messenger arrived with a note. The prince told the dwarfs: "I must return to my father's kingdom. But I can not go on living so far from Snow White. Let me take her coffin and place it in the cathedral of my city, so all may see her beauty."

The dwarfs took pity on the prince and gave the coffin to him.

As the prince's servants carried the coffin on their shoulders down the mountainside, they tripped over a fallen tree. The glass coffin fell and broke. Snow White was thrown out. Her body rolled hard against a tree stump. The poisoned piece of apple, that had been stuck in her throat all those years, was knocked loose and fell out of her mouth.

Before long, Snow White came alive again. She sat up, rubbed her eyes, and cried: "Where am I?"

The king's son, filled with joy, said: "You are with me."

He knelt before her, one hand on his chest, and told her: "I love you more than anything in the world. Come to my father's palace and be my wife."

Snow White saw how handsome he was and said "Yes."

In the cathedral of the prince's city, before a

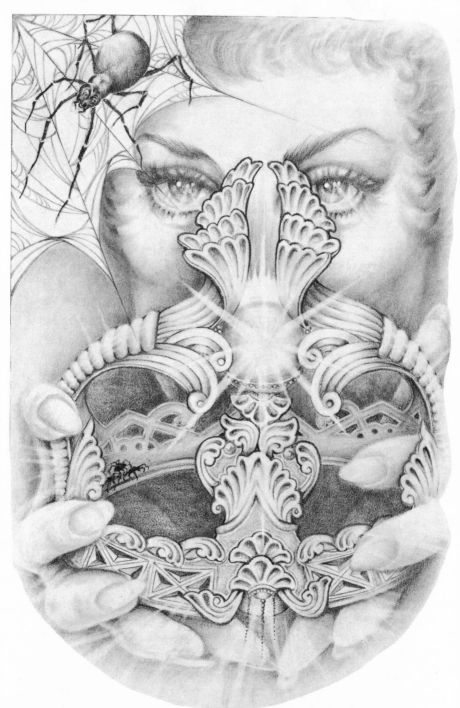

*Illustrated by
Suzan Lovett*

**"Beautiful bride,
accept this wedding gift."**

huge crowd, they were married by the archbishop. Afterwards a great feast was ordered. The prince's father invited kings and queens from everywhere. Even the Black Queen received an invitation.

Trying to decide whether to make the journey, the Black Queen went to the looking glass and asked:

> *"Mirror, mirror on the wall...*
> *Who's still the fairest one of all?"*

To her horror, the voice replied:

> *"Queen, thou hast a beauty rare,*
> *But the prince's bride is yet more fair."*

The Black Queen quivered with rage. "Who can this bride be?" she demanded. Then a smile crept across her face. "I must take her a wedding gift."

So she went to her secret room. By witchcraft she made a beautiful crown of silver and sparkling crystal. But inside it, where a wearer's hair would touch and waken them, she hid four sleeping poisonous spiders. Then, carrying the crown in a box, she journeyed to the feast.

There the Black Queen took the crown out of the box. Carrying it carefully before her, so as not to waken the spiders, she joined the guests.

But when she came forward to offer her gift, she recognized the prince's bride as Snow White, now all grown up. "You!" she said, beginning to tremble with anger and fear.

The crown, slipping from her fingers, fell to the floor. The four spiders waked.

Slowly they began to crawl across the stones toward Snow White.

The prince drew his sword and held Snow White to him.

The dwarfs, who had been watching, grabbed their spades and leaped forward. Down came the spades. Smash! Smash! Smash! One by one, the spiders were killed.

The Black Queen let out a cry of despair. She began running toward the door.

The dwarfs caught her and dragged her back to the fireplace.

"What punishment is proper," they asked, "For a Queen who has tried four times to kill an innocent girl?"

They heated two iron shoes in the flames. When the shoes were red hot, the dwarfs brought them out with tongs and fastened them on the feet of the Black Queen. And in those red hot shoes, she had to leap about until, worn out, she dropped down dead. It was her last dance.

At that moment, in the empty castle of the Black Queen, the magic mirror proclaimed loudly:

> *"In fear no longer need she stand—*
> *Snow White rules fairest in the land."*

And the mirror never spoke again.

Happy and at peace with all the world, Snow White and the prince lived in their palace for the rest of their lives.

Broken Window

In the days of the pharaohs, Egypt was ruled by a governor named Karakoush. He was a short fat man who worshipped the law's wording almost as much as his own power. So—as still happens today—he was kinder to criminals than to their victims.

Now, a man in that country owned a beautiful vase, painted with camels and pyramids. Each morning he would fill it with flowers and place it in his window, so passers-by could enjoy its loveliness.

A thief, seeing the vase, decided to steal it. One night he crept through the man's garden and climbed the house wall. With an iron bar, he began prying the window open. But the frame was weak. Suddenly the wood broke. The thief fell to the ground below, breaking his leg.

The next day, the thief hobbled to the palace. Before Governor Karakoush, he complained: "Your Excellency, I demand justice! I earn an honorable living by stealing. Yesterday I tried to enter the house

Drawing courtesy The Shah Abbas Collection

of this particular man. As I was prying open the window, the frame broke and I fell. See my poor, poor broken leg."

Karakoush shouted to the court guards. The owner of the house was dragged, trembling, before him.

The governor pointed an accusing finger. "Behold this poor thief. You tempted him! Why did you make your window so weak that it caved in, causing him to break his leg?"

What answer could the poor house-owner make? He could see the governor had already made up his mind to punish someone.

So he said: "No, no, it was the carpenter's fault. I paid him to make a window strong enough to prevent such accidents."

Karakoush thundered: "Guards, bring me the carpenter."

The carpenter was dragged before him and accused, with the thief standing smiling beside the governor.

The carpenter crawled forward on his knees, pleading: "Your Wisdom, it wasn't my fault. As I was fastening the window, a lovely woman in a red dress passed beneath me. I was so distracted by the sight I—I drove the nail in crooked."

The woman was found and brought to court.

She answered with a smile: "My beauty is from Allah, who is beyond the reach of your court." The governor's face turned black as fireplace stone. The woman grew pale and added hastily: "But my tailor sewed that lovely dress which caught the carpenter's eye."

"Aha!" shouted Karakoush. "Bring me the dressmaker."

The dressmaker, a very tall thin man, was

pushed stumbling before the governor.

Karakoush said: "You cunning villain. Why did you make this woman's dress so beautiful she would catch the eye of the carpenter? Because he drove the nail crooked, the window frame was weakened and this poor thief fell, breaking his leg!"

The dressmaker stammered one excuse after another. But Governor Karakoush hardly listened. Finally he shouted: "I render judgement. Take this sly criminal out. Hang him in the prison doorway."

Now, the prison door was very low. The dressmaker was so tall his head came all the way to the top. There wasn't even room for a rope.

The soldiers came back and reported they just couldn't hang the dressmaker there, as the governor had ordered.

The thief was outraged. He pointed to his broken leg and demanded: "What about my rights? Is this to go unpunished?"

Karakoush said: "I have pronounced my sentence. It **must** be carried out. Guards, go find a short dressmaker. Hang him instead."

All was done as the governor commanded. The soldiers went out and seized a short dressmaker. Despite his wild protests that he had done no wrong, they dragged him to the prison doorway and hanged him there.

Afterward the thief bowed before the governor. "Thank you, Your Excellency. I see we treat the world alike, you and I. When my leg heals, permit me to bring your wife a suitable gift. I know just where I can find one. You can count on getting a lovely vase, painted with camels and pyramids."

THE FLOWER FAIRY

Once upon a time there was a lonely old woman. She lived in a forest beside a stream. Often she thought: "If only I had a happy young child to keep me company."

So she went to a witch woman's hut and asked: "Can you help me?"

The witch grinned: "No trouble at all, dearie." From her pocket she took a tiny flower bulb. "When Spring comes, plant this. Watch what happens."

The old woman gave the witch a silver piece and took the bulb home.

When the ice had melted off the stream, she planted the bulb in a flower pot. She placed it on her kitchen windowsill in the warm sunlight. Every day she watered it.

Soon, up through the dirt, rose a green shoot. It grew and grew. A bud formed at its top.

One morning the old woman, pleased at how full the bud looked, kissed it lightly. Whereupon the petals magically unfolded.

In the flower's center, on a little green stool, sat a tiny girl. She was fragile and very lovely.

Carefully the old woman lifted her up on the palm of her hand. "Why, you're no bigger than my thumb. I shall call you . . . Thumbelina!"

The living room table became Thumbelina's world. A bowl of perfumed water, peaceful inside a circle of flowers, was her lake. Days the tiny girl would sail happily back and forth on a floating tulip petal. Evenings she would venture out onto the dark table, under the lamp light, to dance for the old lady. Nights she would sleep, on soft moss, in a tiny swinging cradle made from half a walnut shell.

But Thumbelina did not know that out in the garden lived a big toad—slimy, ugly, and all covered with grey warts. Through the window he would watch Thumbelina greedily.

One night the woman forgot to shut the window all the way. When everyone was asleep, in crept the toad. He lifted the walnut-shell cradle onto his back. Taking very small hops—so as not to wake the little girl—he carried her out through the window and across the yard to the stream.

When Thumbelina opened her eyes next morning, she was astonished to see blue sky above her. She peeped over the edge of her walnut shell. "Oh!" she cried.

She was on a large green lily pad floating in the middle of a flowing stream.

Thumbelina, who couldn't swim, thought: "How will I ever get back to my lovely home?"

Just then, up over the edge of the lily pad, rose two bulging eyes followed by a wide green mouth.

"Croak," said the toad. "Good morning."

Beside him rose two smaller eyes. It was the toad's son. He was even uglier than his father.

The big toad said: "Cro-oak! Sing and dance for my son here."

Thumbelina shook her head.

The little toad complained: "Crok! I knew she wouldn't be any fun. She's just a girl. Let's dump her in the water. Maybe she'll kick around and get drownd."

The daddy toad reached out his webbed foot and pushed the little toad under the water.

"Croak," he said to Thumbelina politely. "Please excuse my son's bad manners. I've sent him down to clean your room. Then you can live with us in the mud."

Thumbelina was horrified.

When the toads had left, she crept out on the lily pad to the stream. But there was no way to get across. She began to weep.

Down in the water, the little fishes had heard everything. They never had liked the ugly toads, and they could see how beautiful and sad Thumbelina was. They decided to help her escape.

The fish swarmed around the stem holding the lily pad to the floor of the river. They nibbled and nibbled until it was chewed through.

Down the stream the lily pad floated. At first Thumbelina thought it was fun, the green banks drifting gently by ... But then the stream began running faster. Frightened, the tiny girl climbed back into her walnut shell.

Just then the lily pad hit a sharp rock and split in two. Into the stream splashed the walnut shell.

Dipping this way and that, it bounced against the stream bank and rolled over. Thumbelina was thrown out.

She crawled up the muddy bank. In the blades of

grass—which were as tall as she
was—she knelt and said a thank-you
prayer to God.

Beyond the grass grew bushes. There, out of
string, Thumbelina wove a hammock. She hung it in
an elderberry bush, under a bird's nest which would
keep off the rain while she slept.

Each morning the tiny girl would climb from leaf
to leaf, drinking the dew that had formed during the
night. To eat, she gathered pollen from the flowers.

Her friends were the birds and bees that flew
overhead. And the butterflies—especially the
butterflies. As Thumbelina would dance among the
dry leaves, one would flutter about her in delight. It
had big golden circles on its wings. "I will call you
Sunbeam," Thumbelina said.

One afternoon Thumbelina was playing tag with
Sunbeam. A whole line of grasshoppers stood along
the edge of their little field, watching them. The
lady grasshoppers, who were every bit as big as
Thumbelina, were saying: "What a pitiful-looking
thing she is—see, she has only two legs!" And—
"Why, she doesn't even have feelers on her head!"
And—"Her waist is so thin—ugh, she looks just like
those humans. How ugly she is!"

Thumbelina was so upset she had to run find a
puddle of water, and look at her reflection, to see if
her face really looked that awful.

One day, exploring, Thumbelina came to a
cornfield. Since she was so small, the stalks rose
above her like giant telephone poles. At the edge of
the field was a tree stump. In the rough bark was
set a door no bigger than Thumbelina.

The little girl knocked.

Out popped a lady field-mouse, wearing a white
apron and dust-bonnet.

She squeaked: "Oooh! You gave me such a start. Why, you're only a child. And you look starved. Poor little thing. Come right in. Here, warm yourself by the fire. I'll fix us some hot tea. And cookies. Oh, child, just look at your clothes! They're all ragged. I must find a pretty dress for you to wear."

And on and on she chattered, without stopping to let Thumbelina say a thing.

The mouse-lady invited Thumbelina to come live in the hollowed-out tree stump. So the little girl did. Each day she would clean the rooms and sweep the floor. She also told stories, for the mouse-lady was very fond of stories. Thumbelina was given a big bedroom of her own, with wide windows and yellow curtains.

For a time she was very happy.

But one day the mouse-lady sat Thumbelina down by the fireplace. "Exciting news, exciting news! Soon we shall have a visitor. My Uncle Norway! He's very rich. And he has such handsome black fur. You'll just love him!"

That afternoon, Uncle Norway came for tea. He wore a high black hat and peered down at Thumbelina through black-rimmed glasses.

"My deah," he confided, "I live in a house twenty times this big. My cellar is full of barley and wheat for the winter. And my house is so beautifully dark. It has no windows—I detest sunshine!"

Thumbelina was polite. But she just couldn't like Uncle Norway. Especially when he began to come every tea-time.

After he'd left one afternoon, the mouse-lady babbled: "Dear girl. Isn't it wonderful! He's asked for your hand in marriage. He's quite in love with you. Even if you are—well, you know—only a girl. We must have the wedding right here. By the fireplace. We can start your wedding gown right away. Oh, I mustn't forget to invite all my friends—"

Thumbelina broke in: "But I hate Uncle Norway! His fur is oily. He shivers all the time. And his nose never stops quivering."

The mouse-lady became angry. "Oh fiddle-de-dee! Don't be so stubborn. Or I shall have to bite you with my white teeth. You're lucky to get such a handsome husband. The queen herself has nothing to match his black velvet fur. And he has such a fine dark house."

That night in bed, Thumbelina cried and cried. She thought about running away. But there was a big ditch around the cornfield. Rain had filled it with water. There was no way for her to get across.

Next morning, the mouse-lady hired four spiders to spin and weave cloth for Thumbelina's wedding clothes.

Thumbelina refused to help. She stayed in the yard, bidding farewell to the robins and blue-jays who had sung with her in the forest all Summer. You see, it was turning cold, and the birds had to fly South before Winter.

Finally the day arrived for Thumbelina's wedding to Uncle Norway. The morning was frosty. Thumbelina went out anyway to say a sad good-bye to the beautiful sun. She knew she wouldn't be feeling its warmth any more in Uncle Norway's dark house with no windows.

Lying across the path was a butterfly, stiff from the cold. On its wings were huge golden circles. Thumbelina knelt, her eyes filling with tears. "Please, Sunbeam—don't you leave me too."

Sunbeam's feelers moved feebly. Thumbelina's heart leaped. She lifted the butterfly gently—it was bigger than the little girl, but very light—and carried it on her back into her bedroom. There she laid the butterfly on her bed, where sunshine from the window could warm it. She spread her own blanket, of softest cornsilk, over the butterfly.

During lunch the mouse-lady chattered merrily about plans for the wedding that afternoon. She hardly noticed when the little girl tiptoed away, back into her room.

Sunbeam was up, slowly testing her wings. Thumbelina said in relief: "Oh, Sunbeam, I'm so glad you don't have to die!"

"Oh, but I do," Sunbeam said softly. "Don't you know we butterflies live for only one Summer? At its end we lay our eggs, so next Spring they can hatch into new butterflies."

Thumbelina asked: "And will you lay your eggs soon?"

"I was flying toward the flower garden on the other side of the ditch when the cold made me fall. Thank you, Thumbelina, for giving me back my strength. But now I must be on my way."

Just then, through the window, Thumbelina saw Uncle Norway coming up the road. He was wearing his black wedding suit. Following him was a long line of admiring lady mice.

Thumbelina looked around desperately. "Please, Sunbeam," she begged. "Please! Take me with you!"

The butterfly fluttered its wings. "Yes, I think I'm strong enough. Open the window wide. Then climb on my back."

And out of the window they flew, circling up and up into the beautiful sunshine. Far below, the little

Illustration by
Bella Stoll

girl could see the stump house, and the mouse-lady waving her apron, and Uncle Norway shaking his black cane angrily up at them.

Then the figures shrank away behind them. Sunbeam and Thumbelina went soaring over the ditch.

As the flower garden came in sight, the butterfly's wings beat more slowly. They floated down onto a tall stone fence beside the garden.

The butterfly panted: "I must leave you here. I only have enough strength left to fly to the leaves and lay my eggs."

The butterfly fluttered away. Thumbelina waved good-bye and called: "Next Spring these meadows will be filled with new butterflies, and I will name the prettiest 'Little Sunbeam.' "

Suddenly the tiny girl shivered. Snowflakes had begun drifting down through the cold air. She started searching between the big stones. If she could find a crack, she could crawl in and try to get warm.

Thumbelina could see that most of the flowers down beside the wall were brown and shrivelled. But a clump of gladioli was still in full bloom.

Her foot brushed a pebble off the wall. It fell, bouncing off a gladioli bud. Immediately the flower opened, its inside red as blood.

To Thumbelina's amazement, in the heart of the flower stood a crystal man no bigger than she. He was transparent as clear glass. From his shoulders spread sparkling wings. On his head gleamed a silver crown.

"How beautiful he is!" Thumbelina thought.

She called down: "Who are you?"

The crystal man pointed about him. "In each of these flowers lives a guardian spirit. I am their king. Who are you?"

So Thumbelina told her sad story about the ugly toads, her terrifying journey down the stream, the forest, the mouse-lady, haughty Uncle Norway, and her escape on the back of a dying butterfly.

Looking upward, the crystal man realized she was quite the most beautiful girl he had ever seen. He called: "Come join us. Marry me and be our queen."

Thumbelina was so delighted she hugged herself.

Then she climbed down on a spiderweb that had

frozen, like a silvery ladder, between the fence and the flowers.

From every flower appeared a splendid gentleman or lady fairy, in palace robes of sparkling cloth. Each one bowed to kiss her hand, or curtsied.

The wedding was held amid the flowers. The crystal king took the silver crown from his head and held it above Thumbelina, proclaiming: "So that you may be known by a title that reflects your beauty, I rename you Queen Maia."

There was a sudden shower of snowflakes. When it cleared, only the crystal man remained.

Thumbelina asked: "Your beautiful court—where have they all gone?"

He told her: "Where we too must go."

Taking her hand, the crystal king led her to the center of his flower. Inside it he showed her an opening about the size of their slender bodies.

He explained: "Each flower stem is hollow. It contains a slide that will carry us down beneath the earth, into the bulb from which the flower grows. There, snug and warm, we will wait out the Winter storms. When the snow melts, the flowers will rise up again, carrying us with them."

Thumbelina's eyes closed. She thought of the splendid fairy ladies and gentlemen, already down in their flower bulbs. Tears began to trickle down her cheeks. "You all have such beautiful wings, and I have none. How can I ever be one of you?"

The crystal king said: "Queen Maia, think no longer of yourself as a human being. Just see how much smaller you are, and more fragile. Truly, you are like us—a flower spirit.

"Rest with us. And when Springtime comes, when we rise together into the sunshine, you will find that you too have grown wings, every bit as beautiful as ours!"

And so it happened. During the long Winter, Queen Maia's wings sprouted and grew to full size, strong as the wings of a dragonfly, bright as a dewdrop sparkling in sunlight.

And now, each Summer, a tiny Queen Maia and her crystal king rule over the fairies of their garden kingdom.

So next time you're near a bed of tulips, or lilies, or blooming gladioli, watch!

It's true that if you try to look straight at fairies, you'll never see them, for they hide very quickly. But sometimes, as the grey dusk settles, if you steal a glance out of the corner of your eye . . . you can catch a glimpse of their wings . . . beating.

The Sand Dragon

On the far side of the river stretched a sun-scorched desert. Across this vast sea of sand, like ripples, ran low smooth hills of sand. There the wind was hot, and as dry as your mouth after eating a pepperoni pizza.

But on our side of the river, the country was green, filled with rich farms, wandering goats and palm trees. The sultan—that's what the people called their ruler—lived in a big palace tent, its top white with red stripes. He had thick Persian carpets on the sandy floor, a tea set of finest silver, and chests of fancy clothing.

Even so, fat Sultan Sugafoo was not happy. For back in that desert, in a cave, lived a terrible dragon. Each month Sultan Sugafoo had to give it a maiden to eat or the dragon would attack the country with his fiery breath. And now the time had come to give the monster the sultan's own lovely daughter, Princess Puffaloo.

The sultan shouted: "Never! I will lead my army in war against this dragon! We will chop him into hamburger!"

The sultan's wise men told him: "Don't be a fool. The arrows your soldiers shoot will just bounce off his iron skin. That will make the dragon angry. He will burn up your soldiers with his fiery breath. You, too! Then he'll storm into the palace and eat Princess Puffaloo anyhow."

Sultan Sugafoo said: "Hmmm. Maybe I should hide?"

The wise men told him: "How can you be king and rule the country if you are hiding in a closet somewhere? You belong on the throne."

The sultan nodded: "True, true."

Then he had an idea. On all the palm trees, he had signs posted reading: "Wanted—Someone to kill the dragon. Reward: Half the kingdom and Princess Puffaloo's lovely hand in marriage."

A young man named George said: "Aha!" He was an orphan, learning to be a weaver of cloth. But he was careless—the needles kept pricking his fingers, and he wanted to get into some other line of work. Anyhow, he thought Princess Puffaloo was beautiful, what he could see of her. That was just her dark eyes—she always wore a veil up over her nose.

George stood before the sultan and said: "I will get rid of the dragon for you. Just give me a sword."

The wise men told George: "Useless. Any sword will just break on his iron scales. To fight a dragon, you must use your wits."

Princess Puffaloo wrinkled her eyes at George, which I think meant she was smiling under her veil.

Sultan Sugafoo gave George a dagger, a sackful of dates, three coconuts, and some coconut chip cookies the princess had baked that morning. Only the princess had left them in the oven too long. They were hard and dry as white cardboard.

Off George went, seeking the dragon, across the river and into the desert. He walked three days and two nights, stopping every so often to empty sand out of his shoes. The third night, over the top of a sand dune, he could see puffs of fire, and smoke rising. Can you guess who it was?

Yes, right, the dragon.

When George came over the sand hill, he could see the beast clearly. Its green scales glinted in the moonlight. It stood on two huge legs, tall as a house. Two knobby horns grew over its fierce green eyes. Then came a long nose ending in two bumps that spurted fire when the dragon breathed out.

"Good evening!" George said brightly. "Isn't it dreadfully hot?"

"Humph!" snorted the dragon. It was very nearsighted—it really needed glasses, you know. So it lowered its huge head to George and asked: "Should I eat you? I eat maidens, you know."

George jumped back and protested: "Absolutely not. I'm not a maiden. I'm a young man."

The dragon said: "Too bad." It licked its thick green lips several times and swung its head down again. "I'm very hungry, you understand . . ." The dragon opened its jaws, and by the moonlight George could see it had three rows of sharp teeth on top and four rows on the bottom.

Quickly George pulled open his knapsack. He took out one of the princess' cookies and sailed it, like a paper plate, into the dragon's open month.

*Dragon by
Lonni Lees
Brooker*

"CRUNCH!" went the dragon's jaws. It swallowed and opened its mouth again. Quickly George sailed in the rest of the cookies, one by one. "CRUNCH! CRUNCH! CRUNCH!"

When the cookies were all gone, George showed the dragon the empty knapsack. He asked: "Weren't they a little . . . dry?"

The dragon snorted out two puffs of fire. "Absolutely not! I love things well-done. Can't stand soggy cooking. Well, maybe they could have stood a little more salt."

George nodded: "I'll tell the princess." Then he asked: "Why do you eat maidens?"

The dragon said: "It's a sad story. I have this stomach problem. Too much gas. If I don't eat a maiden every month, I burp. All the time."

George said: "That makes sense. How many maidens have you eaten so far?"

The dragon wiggled the claws on its short front legs, counting. "Let's see, last month was my thirty-sixth birthday. But I didn't start until I was part-way grown up . . . 256, give or take a few."

George said: "I've told you my name. What's yours?"

"Flambeau."

"Isn't that a French word?"

"Of course. My mother was French. I was brought here by a knight in armor—one of the Crusaders, I think they called them. What a fool! Not to know the difference between a dragon egg and an ostrich egg. He buried me in the sand and forgot me."

George said: "So you're an orphan! Just like me. My father was a Crusader too. Only he went back to England before I was born."

Suddenly the dragon burped, sending out billows of smoke. "Excuse me," it said, turning to enter the cave into the sand hill. "I really must get ready."

Then the dragon turned back to George and said: "Since we're almost friends, maybe you'll help me. You don't happen to have any water, do you?"

George shook one of his cocoanuts, and he could hear the liquid sloshing around inside. He asked the dragon: "I thought you hated water."

Flambeau made a face. "I do. It's poison. That's why I need your help. Follow me."

He led George into his cave, deep inside the sand dune. It was dark, but Flambeau lighted the candles by breathing flame on them.

George sat down on the sandy floor. Flambeau showed George the claws on its short front legs. Once they'd been covered with green enamel, but it was all chipped. "Clean it off," the dragon asked.

George took Sultan Sugafoo's dagger, cut open a cocoanut and poured the watery liquid inside into a saucer. Then, very carefully, he painted it onto the dragon's claws.

The instant water touched the enamel, it smoked and bubbled like boiling soup. Flambeau bellowed: "Don't let a drop get on my scales! It'll burn me."

George said: "Don't worry." And when he wiped the claws with a cloth, off came all the green. The claws gleamed in the firelight like white spears.

Flambeau began painting them red. He explained: "They'll look all bloody. Scare the sultan's soldiers away. So I won't have to kill everybody."

George was walking toward the entrance to the cave—walking backward, hoping the dragon wouldn't notice. He said: "Then you're really going to eat the princess?"

Flambeau took an atomizer, sprayed its throat with gasoline, and tried a puff of fire. "Of course," the dragon said. "What else are maidens for?"

By now George was outside the cave. He gave a sob, turned, and ran back across the sand toward the sultan's country.

When George got back to the palace, Sultan Sugafoo was pacing back and forth on his Persian carpet, practicing cuts with his sword. Princess Puffaloo was doing embroidery.

The sultan demanded: "When is the monster coming?"

George said: "Probably tomorrow. He's right behind me."

The sultan bellowed: "We shall fight to the death." *SWISH! SWISH!*

George told him: "Fight any way you want. Just let me talk to the princess." And the young man told her what to do.

"Dragon? Dragon? I'll chop him into hamburger!"

That night they lay awake half the night worrying. All except George. He lay awake **all** the night worrying.

When dawn came, the sultan lined up his archers along the riverbank. He ordered: "Shoot the monster as he crosses."

The wise men gathered on a hill to one side, looking through their magic books.

Princess Puffaloo, wearing her finest robes, stood with proud dignity before the tent palace. In front of her were ten soldiers, her personal bodyguard, holding spears.

From the desert on the other side of the shallow river, the sultan's soldiers could hear the THUMP! THUMP! THUMP! of huge feet coming closer. Above the sand dunes rose a column of smoke and occasional belches of fire.

Then, mounting the last dune toward them, came Flambeau. But when the soldiers saw their enemy, they laughed. Because the monster looked as if it had dressed for a picnic, not for war. Flambeau was wearing black rubber boots, a polka-dot jacket, and carrying an open beach umbrella overhead.

Pretty soon, though, the soldiers stopped laughing. Because no matter how much desert dragons hate water, the river didn't stop the monster. Flambeau just waded across, and those high boots kept the water from touching the beast.

The sultan shouted: "Fire!" All the soldiers shot their bows. But the arrows just bounced off Flambeau's iron scales.

When Flambeau reached the near shore, the dragon lowered its head and looked the soldiers right in the eye. Then the dragon reared back and blew out fire until they dried up like autumn leaves. All except the sultan—he didn't get burned because he was hiding behind his horse. But do you think his knees were shaking?

Bellowing, Flambeau tramped on toward the palace.

On the hill, the wise men and magicians began reciting their spells. The clouds turned black, lightning flashed. Heavy rain poured down.

But did it kill Flambeau? No. The dragon just squatted down on the road, curled its tail around its body, and crouched under the yellow umbrella.

It rained and rained. Until finally the clouds were empty. When it stopped, Flambeau stood up and started once more toward the palace. THUMP! THUMP! THUMP!

The wise men said: "We are defeated. Now the monster will destroy the country. Turn it into a desert."

In Flambeau's path stood a wagon loaded with potatoes. The dragon blew out flames so hot the potatoes all crinked up into dry potato chips.

The princess asked George: "Can nothing stop him? Is he really going to eat me?"

Along the road, behind a fence, a field of corn was growing. Flambeau blew fire over it— "Aggghrrr!" The field exploded into white popcorn, knee deep.

Quickly George ran in front of the princess' bodyguards. He took away their spears and gave them those white plastic circles with long handles you use to blow bubbles. "Dip your circles into this saucer of Ivory Liquid," he ordered.

Flambeau, little flames flickering out of the ends of its nose, bent down to look Princess Puffaloo's soldiers in the eye.

George shouted: "Blow! Blow! Blow!"

Now, you know what the wet part of soap bubbles is made up of. Water!

As those bubbles hit the dragon, and began to melt its green scales, Flambeau roared out in anger. Slapping at the bubbles and shouting "Ahhrrr! Aghhhrrr! Aggghhhrrrr!"

But finally all the liquid was used up. The soldiers had run out of ammunition. Out of bubbles.

Flambeau slashed with his red claws and the soldiers ran away like mice.

George ducked down behind a tent-pole. Princess Puffaloo was alone. She stood very bravely beside a stand on which was a glass vase full of flowers and water.

Flambeau bent down, its eyes closed, and the dragon opened its great jaws to chomp her.

George shouted: "Now, princess! Do it! Do it!"

Calmly, Princess Puffaloo threw away the flowers and emptied the vase into Flambeau's mouth. The water ran smoking down the dragon's long red tongue and into its throat.

How that made the dragon scream! It bellowed and clawed at its neck and rolled on its back on the sandy ground. It knocked down one side of the palace tent and broke six flag-poles. Then the dragon threw its umbrella aside and went racing back to the river and across into the desert, where it sat down and began stuffing sand down its throat.

With the dragon defeated, Princess Puffaloo and George hugged each other. Pretty soon Sultan Sugafoo came limping back and there was a great wedding, with drummers and flute players and dancing girls. Princess Puffaloo and George were married, and he got to rule half the kingdom.

Oh, you want to know what happened to Flambeau? Well, the dragon and George and the princess all got to be good friends. Each Monday, Flambeau would sit at the edge of the river, on the desert side, waiting.

Princess Puffaloo would bake a whole wagonful of coconut-chip cookies. Only she'd forget and burn them. Then she and George would take them down to the river, and one by one George would sail them like paper plates across the water. And Flambeau would snap them up. "CHOMP! CHOMP! CHOMP! CHOMP!"

Afterward George would say: "They were a little burned. Were they all right?"

And Flambeau would roar back across the river: "Fine, just fine. But next time, put in a bit more salt." And Princess Puffaloo would agree.

Only she never did. She always forgot.

The Dragon's Egg

Back before electric lights or automobiles, there was a girl named Margaret who had never had a pet.

Both of Margaret's parents were dead. She lived on a tobacco farm with her Aunt Claudia and her Grandpa Doozer. His real name was Dunkelmann, or something like that, but everybody called him Doozer.

Well, Margaret went to school in a small white wooden building with only one teacher. Margaret was in the second grade. The boys in overalls teased her. And she didn't have any real girlfriends because she was so shy.

After supper each evening, Aunt Claudia would let Margaret play outside before starting her homework. Margaret's favorite place was down past the tobacco field, at the edge of the Great Dismal Swamp.

That swamp was a vast shadowy place, all shallow water with broken reeds sticking out, and flat mud islands. At the swamp's edge, cypress trees twisted their way up, like tall monsters with dry grey moss dripping from their bare arms.

Alligators lived there, for sure. Aunt Claudia often told Margaret: "Now you hear me good, child. You stay 'way from that swamp. Gators swim there. And, some folk say, monsters even more fearsome."

But Margaret liked to slip off there anyhow—not into the dark water, mind you, but walking right up to the edge. She never saw any gators.

One evening she did find a nest, big as a bushel basket, scraped out of the mud. Leading away from it were long footmarks ending in three toes with claws. And in that nest was an egg big as a cantaloupe, wrinkled and sort of greenish-looking.

Margaret looked around carefully. Nothing seemed to be watching her. So she pulled up the bottom of her dress to make a pocket and put the egg in it. Then she hurried home fast as her legs would carry her.

Grandpa Doozer was rocking on the porch, whittling. He called: "What you got there, child?"

Margaret just shook her head. She didn't want Aunt Claudia to know.

Grandpa Doozer coaxed: "Come here. Show me." So she did.

Grandpa Doozer smelled that egg. He tapped it with his fingernail, listening. Then he said: "Never seen nothin' like it, child. Whatever hatches outa this egg, it sure ain't gonna be no gator."

Just then the patched screen door pushed open. Before Margaret could hide the egg, out came Aunt Claudia and saw it. She gave a little yelp and Margaret pleaded: "Kin I keep it, Aunt Claudia? Kin I? Pleeease?"

Claudia said: "No, you kain't. Git rid of it. Now! And then git back in here and start your lessons."

Margaret ran off toward the woods with the egg. But when she got behind the house, she turned off into the chicken coop. She pushed the straw aside and hid the egg under it.

Then she came back to the porch, put her head down like she was sad, and told Aunt Claudia she'd smashed the egg on a rock. Now, Grandpa Doozer was watching her very closely, out of the corner of his eye, and he gave her a wink.

Next day, Margaret moved the egg over to where the sun could warm it. Every night after supper, she and Grandpa Doozer would sneak out and look at it.

Day by day, that egg g r e w . The wrinkles filled out. Gradually it changed color, from green to purple. Gold spots appeared all over it. Grandpa Doozer said again: "Never seen nothin' like it."

Then other colors appeared, specks of orange and white and black. And next day, it *hatched.*

What came out was long as your two hands. It looked a little like an alligator. But it had a pointed tongue that flicked in and out like a snake, and little leather wings. A sharp ridge ran from the center of its forehead down its back to the tip of its tail.

Grandpa Doozer whispered: "Margie girl, you got yourself a r e a l l i v e babydragon. What you gonna call it?"

Margaret said: "Rainbow. Because its skin looks all different colors when the light touches it."

Grandpa Doozer agreed. They tore some newspapers into strips and made a nest for Rainbow.

That night Margaret had a bad dream. Her sleeping place was in the attic alongside the chimney, right under the roof. She imagined she was on a high place, looking down over the swamp. There she could see Mother Dragon, calling softly, searching everywhere for her lost baby dragon.

Next day Margaret sat down beside Grandpa Doozer's rocker for a serious talk about what you feed a baby dragon. Besides milk, that is.

Grandpa Doozer scratched his chin and said: "Well, your Aunt Claudia just peeled a big mess of potatoes. She's got the skins in a cardboard box in the kitchen. Let's try Rainbow on them."

You know, Rainbow loved those potato peelings. The baby dragon ate them all.

It ate the cardboard box, too.

They soon found out that Rainbow loved to eat just about anything. Coffee grounds, banana skins, apple cores, hay, handkerchiefs, buttons, cigarettes . . .

One day Rainbow even ate a cake of soap. That evening, when Margaret came out to the chicken coop, the dragon was asleep. Every time it breathed out, two soap bubbles would form at the end of its long nose, bob loose and float away.

Well, Rainbow grew so fast that she . . . (We have to call Rainbow "she" from now on because Margaret decided it was a girl dragon, although there really was no way of telling.) . . . Anyway, Rainbow grew big as a table. There wasn't room for her in the chicken coop. They had to move her to the back of the barn, into the corncrib.

Of course, Aunt Claudia finally discovered Rainbow. One day there was a scream from the barn. Aunt Claudia came running out, flapping her arms and shouting: "A dragon! A dragon! There's a dragon in the barn!"

Margaret tried to calm her. "Yes'um. It's Rainbow. She's my friend. She won't hurt you."

Aunt Claudia, her face beginning to turn purple, said: "Oh no? Well, that beast came right up to me and before I knew what was happening, look . . . . .
IT ATE MY APRON!"

That night Margaret had a serious talk with Rainbow about good manners. Margaret was sitting in the hay with the dragon's head in her lap, pressing Rainbow's scales flat and scratching behind the dragon's growing wings. Rainbow was looking up at Margaret with her big red eyes and purring like a giant cat.

Margaret said: "Now Rainbow, you must stop scaring people. I know you get nervous, but you'll just have to learn to control yourself. We all get nervous. Look, let me show you what *I* do with my fingers. I make a tapping sound like this." Margaret began drumming her fingernails on the wooden floor. "Now you practice it too. Use your claws."

And soon they were both tapping away, clickety-clickety-click.

Margaret had a special reason for wanting Rainbow to learn how to behave properly. The next day, all the children were to bring their pets to school. Margaret, who never had a pet before, wanted to show off Rainbow.

The next morning, they started off to school together. Margaret looped a rope around Rainbow's neck so the dragon wouldn't fly away. What Margaret had forgotten was that dragons walk v e r y   s l o w l y.

So they were late.

When they finally got to school, Margaret tied Rainbow to a post. Then she went in by herself.

The other boys and girls were already showing off their pets—white mice and hamsters and canaries and turtles and lots of cats and dogs of all sizes. The boy who pestered Margaret the most had brought his big, mean-looking doberman. When he pointed the black dog at Margaret and whispered: "Growl at her!", Margaret felt scared, the way she always did.

The teacher asked: "Margaret, did you bring a pet?"

Margaret answered: "Yes'm. I tied it up outside. It's a dragon."

The boys whooped and hollered, shouting: "Stupid Margaret. Says she's got a dragon. She's too dumb to know what a dragon is! Don't try to fool us. Stupid Margaret. Stupid Margaret! STUPID MARGARET!"

The teacher shook her head and said: "Now, Margaret, we mustn't lie." When Margaret insisted, the teacher got up and said: "Well, I'll just have to go look, you know." And out she went.

As soon as the door closed, the boys began to shout: "Stupid Margaret! Stupid Margaret!"

A minute later, they all heard a scream outside. Margaret knew the teacher had seen Rainbow. Then they could hear footsteps running off.

The boys shouted at Margaret: "Now you're gonna git it!" They began throwing pieces of chalk and erasers from the blackboard.

By now Margaret's eyes were filled with tears. She put up her arms to protect her face and cried out: "Rainbow! Come help me!"

Outside there was a crash as the post broke off. Then the door was knocked flat on the floor. In stomped Rainbow, red eyes glaring, smoke puffing out her nostrils.

The boy crouched over his doberman, pointed at the dragon and ordered: "Sic 'em!"

The dog snarled and leaped at Rainbow.

While the doberman was still in the air, the

dragon opened her mouth and breathed out a huge blast of fire. It burned off the dog's whiskers, his eyebrows, and most of his fur.

The dog, tail between his legs, ran yelping out the door.

One of the blackboards was on wheels. Aiming it like a battering ram, the boys pushed it at the dragon.

Rainbow ATE the blackboard.

Then the dragon tromped slowly across the room, glaring at the doberman's owner with fiery red eyes. Closer and closer . . . until the boy wet his pants and ran crying out the door.

The schoolroom grew quiet as a church.

Margaret wiped her eyes. She tied the frayed rope around the dragon's neck and said: "Let's go home, Rainbow."

She looked around the room, at all the children hiding behind desks or crowded on top of each other in the corners. She pointed her nose up in the air and told Rainbow: "I don't think *anybody* will bother us any more."

When they got close to home, they could see a big circus wagon in front of their house. On the porch, talking with Aunt Claudia and Grandpa Doozer, was the circus ringmaster.

The ringmaster came down. Paying no attention to Margaret, he walked slowly around Rainbow. As he looked, he kept flicking his little whip against his black leather boots. Then he began to whistle to himself, so quiet Margaret could hardly hear him.

At last the ringmaster turned to Grandpa Doozer. "So *that's* your dragon. Quite a beast! Mister, tell you what I'm gonna do. I'll give you two thousand dollars for it."

Margaret shouted: "No! She's mine! I won't sell her!"

Aunt Claudia bent over and said softly: "Listen, child. You know we can't afford to keep a monster like this. It's eating everything in sight. Next thing you know, it'll start on the apple orchard."

Margaret put her arms around the dragon's neck whispering: "Rainbow, show them you won't go."

At that, the dragon roared out a plume of fire. It burned all the paint off the circus wagon, turning it black and smoky.

The ringmaster jumped back. "Well! I see I have to come back tomorrow with a stronger wagon." And he left.

That evening, Margaret was too unhappy to eat any supper. Later she sat in her room with Rainbow's head in her lap, thinking and thinking, what to do. After a while she looked down and saw that Rainbow, who wasn't paying any attention, had eaten her shoelaces.

Margaret knelt up. "Well! I guess Aunt Claudia is right. We can't keep you. But when I think . . . " Margaret took a deep breath and stood up very straight. "No! I won't let that mean old circus put you in a cage. Rainbow—come along with me."

They walked out past the tobacco field. It was dark when they got to the Great Dismal Swamp.

Margaret was a little afraid but she stood on the muddy bank calling into the blackness: "Mrs. Dragon! Mrs. Dragon! I have something for you!"

Far off, Margaret saw two points of light. Closer and closer they came, growing into two great red eyes. When they were right above her in the black sky, two plumes of fire burned down, then faded away in steam.

Margaret said, "Rainbow, go to your mother," and patted the baby dragon on the tail.

Then Margaret looked up at the red eyes and said: "I'm sorry she couldn't stay with me. Maybe she can come visit. Please Mrs. Dragon—take good care of her."

Holding back her tears, Margaret turned and walked home. She didn't look back because she was so sad already.

But later that night, when she was up in the attic under the roof, in her bed beside the warm chimney, she let the tears come. Even after the whole house got quiet, it was hours before she sobbed herself to sleep.

In the middle of the night she was awakened by a thump, as if something heavy had landed on the roof over her head. Next came a scratching sound, like claws walking across the roof. Then the chimney next to her shook a little, as if something were curling around its warm top.

Margaret was filled with hope. She tapped the chimney stones with her fingernails: clickety-clickety-click.

After a minute, from the roof, came the answering sound of claws: CLICKETY, CLICKETY, CLICK!

Margaret knew who was up there. She gave a happy smile. Once more she felt safe and protected.

She pulled the blankets up around her chin and went to sleep.

This is a true story from our own country's history.

About 150 years ago, a man named Henry Wickenburg sailed from his native Austria to the United States. What brought him here was not the promise of freedom, but rather the hope of finding gold—the precious yellow metal that has meant riches for all of man's history.

For many years Henry Wickenburg searched, with horse and burro, through the Western Territories. He panned some low-grade gold dust, and found a few small nuggets. Enough to buy more beans, and dried beef jerky for the trail, and a new pickaxe when his old one wore out.

But Henry Wickenburg never struck it rich. He grew lean as an Apache Indian, his skin burned brown by the sun.

The Civil War was fought in a distant part of America. It meant nothing to Henry Wickenburg. His whole world was the sandy deserts and grey rocks of Arizona, mile after waterless mile. For company he had only the spiny cactus, the crawling gila monsters, and the friendship of his ancient burro, Gretchen.

By 1866, Henry Wickenburg was an old man. His clothing was torn. He had only enough money left for one last grubstake.

He loaded the saddlebags on the back of his ancient burro. They set out from a town so small it didn't even have a name.

Far ahead they could see the granite mountains. Waving his hand toward them, Henry told the burro: "Gretchen, they are too far for us to walk. It would take us a week just to get there. We will have to do our last searching right around here."

Wherever there was a dried-up streambed, Henry Wickenburg would sift through the coarse gravel for the telltale yellow specks. But he found—nothing.

Wherever there was an outcropping of rock, he would break off a piece with his pickaxe, looking inside for the telltale yellow specks. And he found—nothing.

As the days went by, Henry could see that the burro was getting weaker. "Poor Gretchen," he thought. "All these years of toil together, and now I cannot even buy you decent feed."

One day they were heading toward a pile of stones, beside a stream bed that had dried up and was nearly invisible.

Vultures landed on the pile of rock nearby.

The burro stumbled and almost fell.

Henry could see the load was too heavy for the little animal. Quickly he lifted off the saddlebags.

But it was too late. The burro collapsed on the sand.

Henry knelt and cradled the dying burro's head in his arms. Through lips cracked from the sun, he said: "Good-bye, dear Gretchen. In these long lonely years, you have been my only friend. I will stay with you to the end."

At last the burro shuddered and its breathing stopped. Henry bowed his head.

There was a sudden, almost silent sound of wings. Startled, Henry Wickenburg looked up. To see two huge black vultures perched on the pile of rock nearby. As he watched in horror, a third landed.

Henry knew they had come to eat the body of his burro as soon as he left it. In desperation, he shouted at them in his native language. "Go away, du verdampter vogel! Go away!"

But they did not move—huge ugly black birds with hooked beaks for tearing dead flesh.

All of Henry's years of disappointment poured into his voice. "I will not give Gretchen's body to you! With my last ounce of strength, I will bury her myself!"

His fingers groped in the sand. They found a rock. He hurled it at the vultures.

The birds soared up into the sky. Henry's rock hit the pile of stones they had been sitting on and bounced off. One of the stones cracked under the impact. Part of it broke off and fell into the sand.

Henry Wickenburg staggered forward, ignoring the vultures circling overhead. The broken rock lay flecked with gleaming yellow points.

"Gold," Henry breathed. He picked up the broken rock and held it up to the sky, laughing. "Gott in Himmel! Gold. Gold. Gold."

The lode proved to be fifteen feet wide. From it, during the next six years, they took more than $2,500,000 worth of gold. Henry became rich and famous.

And that little town—the one that had no name? They named it Wickenburg in his honor. It lies in Maricopa County, 53 miles northwest of Phoenix. You can visit it if you go traveling. Or find it on your school maps.

Oh, the mine isn't worked any more. They took out 118,000 tons of ore—all of the gold. But the mine, in its heyday, was one of the busiest in all of Arizona.

Henry wanted to name it "Gretchen's Mine." But to all of Arizona's prospectors who knew the story, it had another name. You can still see their title on old maps. They called it "The Vulture Mine."

"Alligator Is Now Playing Second Base"

When I visit other parts of the United States, grown-ups often ask me why I moved to Florida. They laugh: "There's nothing there. Except Disneyworld. And sand."

That's not true. Exciting things happen in Florida. Take that softball game they played in New Port Richie. Most people up North don't believe the story. So at the end of this, I'm printing the newspaper clipping to prove it really happened.

This team of kids went to Pasco-Hernando Community College to play on the practice field. Only they found somebody else was already at second base. An alligator eight-and-one-half feet long. It had crawled up from a nearby swamp.

The coach, Darwin Harmon, said: "Shucks, I'll just push him off the field. Watch me."

So he got into his jeep—it had a low trailer on the back filled with logs—and backed the trailer toward the alligator.

Well, that alligator wasn't about to let anybody steal second base. CRUNCH! It bit off the trailer's tail light.

Coach Harmon said, "Oh-oh!"

He decided to drive back to Dade City—while his

jeep still had four wheels left—and bring one of the men that Florida hires to keep alligators in swamps.

As the coach drove off, he shouted to the kids: "Don't try to play ball!"

But as soon as he was out of sight, you can guess what they decided to do.

Yes, play ball.

One team went out on the field. Their captain studied second base and said: "Guess none of you want to play there." So he sent the extra player out into left field.

The first man up hit a single.

The next batter, a girl, walloped a long fly. It should have been good for at least two bases.

But when she got to first base, the first batter was still there.

She gave him a push and said: "You're supposed to be on second by now. Run!"

He told her: "Not me. I ain't goin' down to second base. You see who's down there? With his mouth open. Look at those teeth!"

She said: "Pooh! Scairdy cat."

"Oh yeah?"

"Yeah!"

He suggested: "You slide down to second base."

"Me?"

"Sure. I'm polite. I let girls go first."

So they both stayed on first base.

By that time, both teams had figured it out. If nobody could get past second base, nobody could score a run. How could either side win the game?

So they decided, just this once, to skip second base. A batter would run to first base, and across the pitcher's mound to third base, and then home.

Along about the third inning, a batter sent the ball bouncing down toward second base.

The alligator was waiting. It grabbed the ball with its mouth. Only it didn't throw to first for a double play.

Instead, the alligator swallowed the ball.

That ended the game.

About then, Coach Harmon came back with the alligator control agent, Mike Fagan.

Mike lassoed the alligator (that's how they catch them). He looped stronger rope around the alligator's tail, and with his truck dragged the alligator tail-first back toward the swamp.

Only the ground was very rough. As the alligator went bumping along on its stomach, it hiccuped or something . . . and coughed up the softball.

"Hey, we can start again," the kids yelled.

They went over and looked at the ball.

It was hardly chewed a bit.

But nobody would touch it.

Would you pick up a ball all covered with greenish alligator vomit?

14B   ST. PETERSBURG TIMES   ■   'THURSDAY, SEPTEMBER 12, 1985

Alligator won't play ball, is bumped from team

By BRUCE VIELMETTI
St. Petersburg Times Staff Writer

NEW PORT RICHEY — A determined alligator forced his way into a tryout at shortstop with a Suncoast softball team Wednesday evening, but was cut despite showing some aggressive defensive play.

Darwin Harmon of New Port Richey said he arrived around 5:30 p.m. at Pasco-Hernando Community College, where his team, Aaro Excavating, was scheduled to practice. On the field, an unlikely player was trying to horn in on a glamor position.

"He was just sitting out there at shortstop," said Harmon, "and he wasn't about to move for us."

So Harmon decided to herd the 8½-foot rookie back toward a swamp about 100 yards from the infield. He backed his Jeep, and a U-Haul trailer heavily loaded with stumps and logs, toward the alligator.

"We figured the trailer would work well," Harmon said, "since it was so low, and you couldn't hurt it." He was only half right.

Proving it wouldn't shy away if forced to cover second in the face of a runner charging spikes high, the gator turned to the oncoming trailer and chomped off a tail-light.

"He was bleeding pretty good from the mouth after that," said Harmon. But the crawl-on candidate still wouldn't leave the field.

"By that time we just decided to play on the other field," said Harmon.

A sheriff's deputy responded shortly, and by about 6:45 p.m. state-licensed alligator control agent Mike Fagan had arrived from Dade City. Fagan harpooned the animal near the edge of the field, tied it up and hefted it into his red pickup truck.

Reprinted from the St. Petersburg Times of Sept. 12, 1985.

Where I Got All These Stories

Ed Sundberg, who let me reprint his Viking poems, is a long-time storytelling friend. They're from his booklet "Temper Not The Wind."

Famed storyteller Ruth Sawyer brought "The King's Flea" back from a trip to Spain. It was printed in 1936 by J. B. Lippincott Co. in "Picture Tales From Spain." Like all the other stories in this book, I've changed it some.

"The Snake King's Gift" was put together from ideas in several other stories. You might want to compare it with "The Language Of Beasts" and "Lucky Luck" in Lang's "Crimson Fairy Book."

Three of the stories are based on folktales collected by the Brothers Grimm. I've switched the emphasis in "Snow White" and added a new twist to the ending. "Princess Briar Rose" is guided to maturity by new rhymes. And I combined the best parts of three Grimm tales—they all have the same plot—for "The Seven Ravens."

An inn-keeper in Devonshire, England, ruined a night's sleep for me—his bed was lumpy, too—with "The Creeping Skulls." I've never seen it in print before.

"The Faithful Tiger" has roamed the jungles of Southeastern Asia since the days of Buddha. You can see how Lotta Carswell Hume tells it in "Favorite Children's Stories From China And Tibet," published in 1962 by Charles E. Tuttle Co.

"The Cream Witch" has many relatives, like Italy's Strega Nona, or Mickey Mouse as the sorcerer's apprentice in the movie "Fantasia." My grandfather Otto Bradl, who told me about Nidelgret, was from Bavaria. But I like the landscape used by Fritz Meuller-Guggenbeuhl in his "Swiss-Alpine Folk Tales" published by Oxford University Press in 1958.

Tales of self-effacing holy men exist in all cultures. "The Emerald Lizard" has run a glittering trail through much of Central and South America. A telling in Spanish, by Carlos Samayao Chinchilla, is the basis for the version in "Ride With The Wind," published by Whittlesey House in 1955.

"Broken Window" has been told for thousands of years in India and the mid-East. This is the Egyptian version. You'll also find it in "Arabian Romances and Folk Tales" by Habib T. Katibah, published by Charles Scribner's Sons in 1929.

"The Flower Fairy" is the very first story I ever told. There are tales of tiny people in every country. This is my version of Hans Christian Andersen's "Inchelina."

I made up "Sand Dragon" and "The Dragon's Egg."

Two stories really happened. "Alligator Now Playing Second Base" adds details to a story printed in the St. Petersburg (FL) Times on Sept. 12, 1985. The history of "The Vulture Mine" also is told in a pamphlet "From The Ground Up" printed in 1981 by the Phelps Dodge Corporation.

The illustrations were created by a talented crew of artists—Gail Bennett, Lonni Lees Brooker, Leslie Ferrara, John Horrall, Carol Jenkins, Suzan Lovett, and Bella Stoll—who live across the U. S. but who all share my sense of fantasy. Rob Bovarnick did the photographs.

Behind The Book

This book was created for the Ruth Sawyer Memorial Foundation. It's part of their Oral Literature In The Schools program. Many teachers and media specialists are expected to read the tales aloud during school storyhours.

The book's creator, Ralph Wallenhorst, is the foundation's Designated Teller. He's opened the Shining Gates of Fairyland to students in schools from Boston to San Diego and from Minneapolis to Miami. He also conducts workshops for teachers. Before becoming a professional storyteller, he was a prize-winning newspaper reporter and magazine editor.

RUTH SAWYER was America's most popular storyteller of the early 1900s. Born in Boston, she grew up amid folktales brimming from her Irish nanny, Johanna. An adventurous child, she also tagged along with her four older brothers on sailing, camping and hunting trips. In 1900, when she turned 20, she was in Cuba organizing kindergartens. She earned her bachelor's degree from Columbia University at 24, then spent three years in Ireland as correspondent for The New York Sun. She became a professional storyteller and lecturer in 1908; during the next half-century, she was to give thousands of performances. At age 31 she married a physician; they had a son and daughter.

Ruth Sawyer's 34 books won her the Newbery Medal, the Laura Ingalls Wilder Medal, and the Regina Medal. Her "Way Of The Storyteller," still in print, is a Bible for present-day storytellers. She died just short of her 90th birthday. Probably she's now ensconced on a grassy mound just inside the Pearly Gates, beguiling St. Peter—and probably St. Patrick—with tales of fat kings and feisty leprechauns.

Plate by Lonni Lees Brooker

Did You Borrow
This Book?

If someone did lend it to you, probably you'd like a copy for your very own.

Try your bookstore first. If they don't have it, you can buy "Ralf's Stories" by mail.

For the paperback edition, send $7.50 to: Dragon Tale Press, Post Office Box 86255, Madeira Beach, FL 33738. (That's $6 for the book and $1.50 for handling, postage, and sales tax.) Be sure to print your name and address so your book doesn't get lost on the way.

For a hardcover version—it makes a wonderful birthday or Christmas gift—send $13.50 to the same address.

Special discounts are offered to educational systems or for bulk purchases.